S & M

AND OTHER STORIES

S & M

AND OTHER STORIES

ROBERT MICHAEL AUSTIN

BLUE MOON BOOKS
NEW YORK

S & M:
And Other Stories

Copyright © 2007 by Robert Austin

Published by
Blue Moon Books
An imprint of Avalon Publishing Group, Inc.
245 West 17th Street, 11th floor
New York, NY 10011

First Blue Moon Books Edition 2006

ISBN-10: 1-56201-522-2
ISBN-13: 978-1-56201-522-0

9 8 7 6 5 4 3 2 1

Printed in Canada
Distributed by Publishers Group West

CONTENTS

FOREWORD

I'm not big on offering advice to tourists. Yet, when pushed, I will tender three "nevers" for Mexico:

Never go out in the peak sun hours.

Never drink the water.

Never pay more than 200 pesos for a lap dance.

Fortunately, as I understand my brief, it isn't to aid travelers or point them toward the most interesting archeological ruins—it's to say a few insightful words about Mexican prostitutes. They are, after all, the theme of these stories.

The Brits call a man who is an authority on a given country an old hand—i.e., *an old India hand*. So, I suppose, after living in Mexico off and on for the last forty years, I'm *an old Mexico hand*. That, plus my squandered life in general, surely qualifies me to comment on these ladies.

I like to think of Mexican prostitutes as *putas milagrosas*, for they are truly miraculous, in that they possess abilities that sometimes transcend the laws of nature and always transcend preconceived notions of what their talents should be. The stories comprehend this. Want to know the secret of the flat-chested whore's unorthodox success? Read the story. How it is possible for one whore to enslave all the prominent men in town? In what way does a deaf whore foretell the future? How does a young whore help an artist obtain just the right colors for his painting of her? All through miraculous ways, I can assure you. Can you just imagine a chippy in Chicago or a doxy in Denver performing feats of legerdemain? Of course you can't. You have to come here to Mexico for that sort of thing. The author of these stories obviously knows his way around. (He claims the stories are based on fact, which I am inclined to believe.) That most of the stories take place in the Yucatan, my old stomping ground, is particularly appealing. It's a magical place to begin with.

Even if Mexican whores aren't miraculous in the sense I've described above, their beauty alone would make them extraordinary. I have often pondered how Mexico has so consistently created exceptionally beautiful women, "the most beautiful women in Christendom." The author must have pondered this as well, but, unlike me, he has figured it out. In one of the stories he solves this mystery once and for all.

I'd like to say a final word about one of my favorite expats—the Emperor Maximilian. OK, sure, he made a couple of mistakes. (One of which was he brought his wife, Carlota, with him. In fact, she figures prominently in one of the stories.) His biggest mistake was probably that firing squad. But Max had an eye for Mexican women. Don't we all.

Arthur Standin
San Miguelito, Mexico

S & M

꧁꧂

We Mexican men aren't masochists, as a rule, although apparently there are enough of us to afford a living to a few professional sadists—a dominatrix as these women call themselves when they advertise. Mistress Xylina was easily the most successful of them and the reason for her success was quite simple: she was the cruelest of them all.

I should tell you about the day I became her slave. Upon entering her apartment (it was in Tlatelolco, one of the last areas in Mexico City where one could still find a large apartment; moreover, it was convenient as I could walk there from the Foreign Ministry) she demanded that I drop to my knees and crawl over to her. She was wearing a red leather dress, four-inch heels that I would happily have polished with my tongue, and carrying a riding crop. I inched over to her, keeping my head close to the floor as I knew I was unworthy of looking my mistress in the eye. I was worried, of course, as I'd been told that she could be without pity.

She spat at me. "You sniveling little worm, tell me what you want most in life. Tell me your deepest desires."

I hesitated—my head was still touching the floor. Then I said, truthfully, desiring this more than anything I could imagine: "Mistress, I want you to beat me! I beg you to whip me! Hit me! Kick me! Hurt me!"

I was about to learn just how cruel she could be. She smiled and said: "No."

THE ARTIST

One fine day an artist arrived in Progreso. It was a day of no other significance, and that assumes, of course, that you believe an artist in your midst is significant in the first place. The artist found it easy to rent one of the small houses that sit on the beach facing the *Golfo de Mexico*, for the town had not yet been transformed by Mexicans with too much money to spend and American expatriates with too much time on their hands.

I didn't know the Progreso of those days, but I do remember it from old photographs and postcards. Because 1950's photos are almost always in black and white—well, if you think about it old photos are mostly in tones of gray—I can't think of the town as having had color. I can still visualize those souvenir postcards with the fancy type that read *"Ven a Descubrir Progreso"* which was superimposed over pale gray clouds and a gray sky, and below the sky the deeper gray of the gulf—and that lower gray swatch of the picture that town officials hoped we could imagine was sand on a beach. Yet I know the artist must have admired endless cerulean skies; honey colored sand; orange, pink, and blue houses as he walked into town; the red dresses the whores wore. Yes, the old photos of Progreso have misled me—for his paintings of that period are the most colorful of his career, and he was a man who painted what he saw.

He had arrived by bus and he returned from the empty house to the station to begin carrying the numerous cardboard boxes he had brought with him. The number of boxes was not unusual for, in those days, families often moved all their earthly possessions by bus. But most of the boxes he had brought with him contained paints, brushes, canvas, stretchers, oils and turpentine, and charcoal and paper for sketching. It took him three trips to carry his possessions to the house.

The whores in town had noticed his frugality—the taxis at the station had offered their services to no avail—and dismissed him as a not very worthy prospect. But Catalina, the youngest of the whores, thought he was handsome. She was still young enough to believe that things like "handsome" mattered when it came to men.

The whores saw him again when he went to a store to buy a bed and mattress, two chairs, and a table. He must have found the empty house despairing—or he was simply tired from his earlier labor—for this time he paid a taxi to deliver the purchases. But by then the whores had tired of watching him and had already gone back into the cantina and missed seeing this apparent extravagance.

The artist—a recent graduate of the School of Fine Arts in Mexico City—had decided he was going to change the course of art in Mexico. But he couldn't do it by remaining in Mexico City, for the young artists there had decided that abstract expressionism, which had taken over American art and then European art and was now devouring Mexican art, was unstoppable.

The older artists he admired, such as Raul Anguiano, Manuel Gonzales Serrano, Gabriel Fernandez Ledesme and Fernando Leal, were considered hopelessly old fashioned. Even Diego Rivera was no longer influential. In a drawer at the school he had discovered a group of drawings by Alfredo Ramos Martinez. They were a revelation. They were drawings of Malinali, the woman some believe was a princess who was sold into slavery, but others believe was the first prostitute in Mexico.

The artist had thought: how can someone look at the face of this Mexican woman and still wish to paint like Jackson Pollock or Franz Kline, rather than Alfredo Martinez? At his school library in Mexico City he had gotten a book on Mexican history and learned that Malinali had been a Maya, a Yucateca, and a week after he graduated he caught a bus to Progreso.

So important was his mission to rescue Mexican art that he wasted no time and was in the cantina that first evening with his sketch pad in hand. It was a dismal place—it may possibly have had a wooden floor under all the dirt and crud on it—but it was the cantina that the whores seemed to prefer. They came and went, picking up a man whenever possible, but they spent most of their time drinking cerveza when there were no men interested in them. He spent the evening sketching the whores—from a distance—for they, more than ever, thought he wasn't worth their time. They could tell from his haircut and his clothes that he was from one of the big cities—but that didn't mean he would spend any money on them. The other patrons—all men, for there were no women except whores who came into the establishment— found his sketches "*muy real*" and "*simpatico*" as they peeked at them over his shoulder. Catalina, the young whore who thought he was handsome, was unfortunately occupied with a sailor from Venezuela and didn't make it to the cantina that night.

Discouraged, he spent the next day going through the sketches before he admitted that none of the whores from the night before could be his modern Malinali. He spent a few hours on the beach—after all, that was one of the reasons for choosing Progresso—before he walked into town to find a café where he could take his evening meals.

At the cantina that evening all the other whores were teasing Catalina for having missed the handsome artist.

"He begged me to pose for him," one of them said.

Another said, "He couldn't take his eyes off me! I think he wants to marry me."

Catalina couldn't believe her bad luck. First, the Venezuelan sailor had refused to give her a tip, and now she learned that the other girls had a head start with the artist. Furthermore, the artist decided to spend that evening stretching canvasses and didn't leave his house while Catalina refused two perfectly good offers so as to not miss him if he came in.

Ah, but the next night! The artist was seated at a table at the cantina, nursing a bottle of cerveza and doodling in his sketchbook, when she came in. Her face had those quintessential mestiza features: beautifully large dark eyes, full red mouth, high cheekbones, dark and glowing hair which she parted in the center to let it fall on her shoulders. Her body hovered between that of a girl and a woman. Her legs were long and slim but her hips and rear were mature. Her breasts were still small, although they were as animated as jumping beans. She was wearing her favorite red rayon dress, which was so shiny it might have been on fire.

She would later tell him she saw him first but, in truth, they saw each other at the same time for he stood up, his heart pounding, as she walked over to him. Inexplicably, a dove flew in through the open door and hovered over their heads. No one had ever seen a dove—or any other bird, for that matter—in the cantina before. At the same time, the radio abruptly changed stations, on its own for no one was near it, and began playing *Solo tu*, a popular love song of the time. As if that weren't enough, the Venezuelan sailor—a jealous man who loved a good knife fight—had been on his way to the cantina to insist that she spend the night with him again, but he slipped on a banana peel someone had carelessly left on the sidewalk and was knocked unconscious for three hours.

They exchanged names. He—Lucien. She—Catalina (OK, so it says Ursala on her birth certificate). He—twenty-five. She—fifteen (OK, this time her birth certificate got it right). He quickly agreed on her price for the night. If you think about it, she might have given him a small discount, for the dove was determined to follow them home, which was a good sign, but then she had rent to pay.

They walked arm and arm to the house, but when they got there she learned he had no interest in making love. Instead, they spent the night talking—while he sketched her over and over again. Each time she moved toward the bed—for she wanted him between her legs—he would say, "Hold that pose a little longer!" Her pussy, which her customers found to be as sweet as a papaya, went untasted that night.

The next day the girls asked her what the artist had been like.

"He was like a madman," Catalina said. "We made love perhaps twenty times. Each time I tried to get out of bed he would pull me back and say, 'I must have you again.'"

"Did he never go soft?"

"No, never."

"When will you see him again?"

"Tonight. He said he will beat me if I go with another man."

"Oh!"

"Yes, he actually did beat me just to show me what to expect."

"He must love you very much!"

She was with him every night for the next two weeks and each night was the same as the first one. Although he didn't touch her, each morning he paid her the amount they had first agreed upon. He was pleased with his sketches and was ready to paint a large nude of her, in the style of Goya's *Maja Desnudo*. He liked the symbolism in choosing that pose, for the majas, in Goya's time, were street girls; not necessarily prostitutes, but certainly girls who lived by their wits.

The next night he began blocking in the painting, building the undertones of color. He expected it to ultimately become the finest nude painted in Mexico in decades. A painting that would stop Jackson Pollock in his tracks. Catalina lay back on his bed in that Goyaesque pose, languid and voluptuous, with her arms pulled back so her hands were behind her head, and her breasts were lifted. Her pussy, exposed to him as she lay nude, remained unemployed, however, although what she really wanted was for him to throw his brushes on the floor and climb on top of her and demonstrate some serious artistic behavior.

He needed daylight to complete the painting so he negotiated the price for her to come during the day as well as for a few hours at night.

"Oh, yes!" she replied. "I'll cook for us!" She brought pots and pans from where she lived and shopped at the market each morning on the way to his house. She learned which meals were his favorites and, within a few weeks, he began to put on weight. At school he had been considered somewhat skinny.

Her new schedule was such that she seldom saw the others girls. But once, while getting up from posing on the bed, she accidentally bumped against the iron headboard, which left a bruise on her left temple. (He was too distracted while blending some yellow ochre and burnt umber to even notice.) And that presented a good excuse for her to look up the other girls. When they saw the bruise, Catalina said, "Oh, that? Lucien saw me looking at another man and he struck me."

And the girls replied, "Oh, Catalina, we wish we could find a man who loved us that much!"

One day, while painting her arms, he became frustrated. "There are delicate green shadows but I can't get them right!" he complained.

She got up from posing and came over to the large canvas. She studied the painting for a moment, then said, "Do you have any oxide of chromium?"

He searched through his paints. "No!" he said. "But you're right, that's just the color I need."

"There are no art supply stores in Progreso, but I'll make some at home tonight."

The next morning, when she arrived at his house, she was carrying a small pigskin bladder containing the chromium mineral, which she had ground until it was suspended in a fine oil. When he added the paint to the shadow areas it was the perfect color and her arms took on the tonality he desired.

The same thing happened when he was painting her legs. "Your legs have some delicate yellow shadows that I can't get right," he said.

She got up from posing and walked over to the large canvas. After studying it for a moment she said, "Do you have any aureolin dore?"

He searched through his paints. "No!" he said.

"I'll make some tonight," she replied.

The next morning she came in carrying a small pigskin bladder with the aureolin mineral suspended in a fine oil. "Your hands are all scratched," he said. "And there is dirt under your nails."

"I had to dig deeper than I expected to find the aureolin," she replied.

When he added the paint to the shadows on her legs they took on a roundness that made you want to touch them.

His next frustration came when he tried to paint her lips. "You don't understand them well enough," she said. "Come over here and kiss them. It's the only way to truly understand their texture and shape." He kissed her for a long time and he agreed, after they broke for air, that he understood her lips now in a way he couldn't have known before.

He went back to painting her lips and he was immediately able to improve their shape, but the color still wasn't right. She got up from posing and walked over to the large canvas. She studied it for a moment and said, "Do you have any rose quinacridone?"

He searched through his paints. "No!" he said. "But you're right, it's just the color I need."

"I'll make some when I go home tonight," she said.

The next morning, along with bread, cheese, and fruits from the market, she handed him a pigskin bladder with the quinacridone mineral suspended in a fine oil. When he added the paint to her lips they came to life and were—almost—as kissable as the originals.

Next he began painting her breasts. He became frustrated when he couldn't get their shape just right. "Come over here and kiss them," she said. "It's the only way to understand their texture and shape."

He spent a wonderful hour kissing them and sucking gently on her nipples. He was certain he understood them well enough to return to the painting but she kept him there kissing them another hour just to be sure. Indeed, when he made the changes to the painting their shape was exactly right. But the color wasn't. She got up from posing and came over to the large canvas. She studied it for a moment and said, "Do you have any alizarin crimson?"

He searched through his paints. "No!" he said.

"I'll make some at home for you tonight," she said.

When she arrived the next morning she was carrying another pigskin bladder, this one containing the crimson mineral suspended in a fine oil. He noticed an ugly bruise on her arm and inquired about it. "I was chipping the alizarin from an outcrop of ledge and I accidentally hit my arm with the hammer," she said. When he added the paint to her nipples they suddenly looked as lovely as ripe cherries.

In the Goya painting, as you know, the *maja* has her legs pressed together—but Catalina preferred to leave hers openly parted. This improved the design of the painting considerably. After all, she had learned a few tricks in the cantina. She had anticipated his need for a black that would do justice to her pubic hair. For she had noticed that the only black he had in his supplies was an ivory black, which she considered much too dull. That night, at home, she took a piece of obsidian and ground it until it until it was suspended it in a fine oil, and she delivered it to him the next morning in a pigskin bladder.

He noticed her leg was swollen. When he inquired about it she said, "When I was out in the desert searching for the obsidian a snake bit me. But, don't worry, I got the poison out."

The painting went along well from there until he arrived at that most important area: her *maja* vagina. She had known this area would be difficult to paint but, since she had been anticipating it for some time, she knew just what to do. Indeed, he soon discovered he couldn't get its delicate shape right—nor could he convey the softness of her pubic hair, although the obsidian black was perfect.

"Come over and touch me between my legs," she said. "It's the only way to understand the texture and shape of my *panocha*."

He put down his brushes, walked over to where she lay on his bed, hesitated, then buried both hands in her sweet sweet snatch. One suspects he then went on to find other ways to understand her texture and shape.

When he had finished painting her vagina, depicted in graceful strokes of color that ranged from rose madder to cobalt violet, it was as inviting as a spring garden where a man might choose to lie down to forget all his earthly troubles. He portrayed this treasure between her legs as both primal and neoteric, as virginal and wicked, as a temple and an opium den—as a place of refuge for Venezuelan, Argentine, and Panamanian sailors as well as a refuge for an artist searching for truth and beauty.

Some critics have said that the strokes of magenta quinacridone on her labia major are brilliant; unequaled in all of Mexican art. I don't profess to know whether or not the twenty centimeters or so of paint and canvas that compose her vagina are among our greatest artistic achievements. I am a mere amateur—a dilettante—so when I say I believe it is her face with its ochre and umber tones, eyes as black as marbles, and ruby lips, that are the true heart and soul of the painting, you may choose not to believe me. But consider this: wasn't finding such a face his sole reason for traveling to the Yucatan?

Later—for the final touches—he worked in a view of the gulf as seen through a window in the room behind her reclining figure.

Now that I've added that final detail, of course you recognize the painting. You have seen it a hundred times before at the *Museo de Arte Moderno* here in Mexico City. You may remember that it hangs just to the right as you climb the grand staircase up to the second floor. If you take the elevator—as I do these days—then you will remember it from another direction. There's usually a crowd. People are amazed that one artist could paint anything so lovely. They are amazed when they see the quality of the other paintings the artist did of Catalina during his lifetime. It is indeed sad that his life's work was so small, but it took him an inordinate amount of time to complete a painting. His working methods remain a secret. His widow—who returned to the Yucatan after his death here in the capital—doesn't grant interviews.

OFELIA

When Ofelia was fifteen she took up whoring. As it happened, she fell
in love with her very first customer. That isn't usual, but it's not unheard
of. Each day she hoped he would return, for she had put her heart and
soul (as well as her ass) into the hour they were together.

This longing for him went on for four years.

Every time she saw a man in his forties approach her, her heart would
leap since it was possible, wasn't it, that it was him? (Without her
glasses, her eyesight was so poor the man had to get to within about six
feet before she could be sure.)

Then one day she saw his picture in a movie magazine. He was about
to star in a major movie. She was surprised to learn his name was different than the one he had given her. Nevertheless, she was thrilled and
filled with hope. She had a friend take a photo of her and she wrote a
note to him and sent both in care of the movie studio in Mexico City.
She poured out her love for him, using the kind of florid language a
movie star might be expected to want to hear. Being practical, she also
reminded him who she was (just in case he didn't recognize her) and she
apologized for charging him that first time but said that all future times
they got together would be free of charge.

She heard nothing from him.

Then one day another movie star picked her up. She recognized him
easily enough for she was now reading movie magazines exclusively.

(She had taped a hundred pictures of her lover on the walls of the room she rented, all of them torn from such magazines.) She couldn't wait to get to a nearby hotel because she wanted to ask this man if he knew Fernando B—, the man she loved.

When they were in the room, she asked him.

"Yes, of course I know him. Why do you ask?"

"I was hoping he would visit me."

"Has he ever?"

"Only once."

"How old are you, chica?"

"Nineteen."

"Well, that's the problem, isn't it?" the man said as he moved behind her on the bed in order to position her on her hands and knees in front of him. "It's well known that Fernando only likes fifteen-year-old girls."

THE FLAT CHESTED WHORE

The interview went badly. Although the *putanero* was moved by the young girl's urgent need to earn money to support her invalid mother and five younger sisters, he felt the girl possessed little beauty. She was too plain to be desirable to the brothel's clients. Yet she appeared enthusiastic and, he thought, could likely be taught to satisfy all sorts of nasty perversions. No, he discarded that idea. She wasn't even pretty enough for that. (He remembered when men used to be satisfied just to climb between a girl's legs. Now they wanted to do things that made him shudder.) He apologized and called for an older whore—who acted as his assistant—to escort her out. But then another idea occurred to him and he had a quick whispered conversation with the woman before she told Carmelita, the young girl, to follow her.

"What was his decision?" the older whore asked as they walked, pretending she didn't know.

"I'm not pretty enough to work here," the girl answered sadly. But the girl didn't curse her bad luck, as most would have. She never blamed God for her lack of beauty. In His wisdom He had chosen her body and her face and that was that.

"It's true, you're not," the older whore reluctantly agreed. Her elegant high heels went click click on the tile floors.

"He said if only I had large breasts then they might compensate for my plain face."

"Yes, men love large breasts and will overlook many faults to get their hands on them."

"Besides my plain face I also have a flat chest, as you can see." She lowered her head in embarrassment.

The whore reached out and tweaked the girl's tiny nipples through her thin blouse. "You are no larger than a boy." (Actually, the older whore had a penchant for girls who were androgynous—but that was another matter.)

"I know."

"This establishment has a reputation to uphold. The *putanero* must be very particular."

"I've heard if you let a black sheep suckle on you it will increase your size. Do you know if that is true?"

"Yes, that is a proven method. Unfortunately, it will also turn your milk black. That is why so few women choose it. The color will have no ill effect on the benefits of your milk, but your children may be traumatized."

That information left the girl uncomfortable and speechless.

"It also takes a long time and sheep are smelly," the whore continued. "There are doctors, of course."

"Yes?"

"It is called breast augmentation."

"Augmentation?"

"It's a medical term that I assume means bigger. There is a man in Merida who performs such operations. But he charges 100,000 pesos."

"Is there that much money in the world?"

"I may know of another way to help you." The woman stopped walking so she could have the young girl's complete attention. "Did you know that each time a woman makes love to an ugly man her breasts increase in size?"

"No?"

"Yes, in both circumference and weight. They increase in size each time. The increase is small—yet cumulative. I'm sure if I talked to the *putanero* and told him you were willing to service the ugly men who come to our door, then he would consent to giving you employment."

"Would you do that for me?"

"Of course. And you'll be bigger in no time."

"But does that method always work?"

"It has never failed."

"Why don't women with ugly husbands develop large breasts?"

"Think, Carmelita, how often do they make love to their husbands? Once or twice a week? Less if they can get away with it? That doesn't create enough of that particular magic inside your breasts to help them grow."

"And if my breasts became truly large?" There was excitement in her voice.

"Then with a little make-up on your face, I'm sure you could make the transition to servicing the kind of desirable clients the rest of us have."

"I would like that."

"I'll be frank in telling you that most ugly men, amputees, and the otherwise deformed, are turned away from the brothel, for the girls fancy themselves too elegant to let such men climb into their beds. This is a shame, as I'm sure you must agree."

"Of course, they must need love more than anyone."

"I can tell you're a sensitive girl."

"Are the men truly ugly?"

"Prepare yourself, Carmelita."

So, it came to pass that Carmelita was installed in a back room on the main floor. The room—which had been used for storage of beans, potatoes, and canned goods until it was emptied and cleaned and set up with a small bed—was chosen because it was off a hallway that was close to the rear entrance to the brothel. Her clients could visit her without having to present themselves at the main entrance.

Word of young Carmelita's availability spread among the disfigured, the deformed, the ugly, the ghastly, the cadaverous, the repulsive, and the loathsome men of the surrounding towns. They were delighted when they heard the news.

At first everything went smoothly, but soon the hallway was so crowded with men who were waiting their turn that it was impossible for any of the other employees of the brothel to use it. So the *putanero* had a carpenter build a series of benches that would seat twenty men, and he placed the benches outside in the patio. Numbers were painted on each seat—one through twenty—so each man could take his place in line without the arguments that had taken place in the hallway as to who had arrived there first. When it was a man's turn to go inside all the others would get up and advance to the next seat, somewhat like the children's game of musical chairs. When twenty seats turned out to be inadequate the patron had another ten made.

But the benches were hot in the sun during the day and when it rained only the truly pitiful chose to remain, willing to becoming soaking wet rather than miss a chance to be with Carmelita. Since the venture with Carmelita was extremely profitable, the carpenter was called back and the area with the benches was enclosed by four walls, a flat roof, and an open doorway. It was nothing more than a large shed but the addition was welcomed by the men.

In the meantime, Carmelita had made her room cozy by adding a chair, a mirror, and numerous pictures of Our Lady of Guadalupe. She also swept the room each morning, without fail, and changed the sheets after every tenth customer. She was surprised at how quickly she adjusted to the unusualness of her clientele. One man always pulled a stocking over his face so she wouldn't have to look at him. She was never able to coax him to remove the stocking although after they got to know each other they chatted like old friends. But most of the hideous made no attempt to hide their disfigurements. They had long grown tired of doing so. One man always had his nephew accompany him for the nephew was a strong boy and could lift his uncle out of his wheelchair and place him between her legs. When the man was finished he would turn to his nephew who would come over to the couple and put his arm around his uncle's thin waist and lift him from between her legs and place him back in the wheelchair. The nephew was a polite boy who never interrupted the couple by coughing, spitting, or complaining that his uncle took too long.

A year passed and Carmelita's breasts had increased in size from 30a to 34b. When she presented herself to the *putanero* and proudly removed her bra, he was quite pleased with what he saw.

"In another year, Carmelita, I've no doubt your breasts will have increased to such a size to merit your promotion to one of the upstairs rooms. Keep in mind, however, that your current earnings equal those of our very best girls and surpass the lazier ones."

A second year passed and when she presented herself to the patron she measured 38d. He ran his hands over her to make sure there was no trickery involved. But they were true, firm, plump breasts with particularly lovely rose colored nipples.

"Alright," he said. "You may leave the downstairs room and join the other girls. But I have one request to make. Stay one more month downstairs so you can inform all your loyal customers that you will be leaving them and that they are no longer welcome here."

So, when she informed each man of her plans, each one begged her to stay. They made outrageous promises to her, promises she knew they wouldn't keep, such as a willingness to bathe and shave more often—but she was nevertheless deeply touched. Some threatened to do away with themselves, which is a grave sin for which she felt she would be partly responsible, or they threatened to turn to a life of crime in their despair. Wouldn't she please reconsider?

At the end of the month she admitted to the patron—who feigned surprise—that she couldn't leave her clients since all 200 of them loved her so much.

At the end of the third year she was a 48dd.

By the end of the fourth year she was a 60hhh.

At 60hhh she began to experience difficulty walking, for her breasts, while she was vertical, hung past her waist and swung side by side causing friction and soreness, or they banged against each other and into people who were near by, and they were, in general, a nuisance. But they were also her fortune so she never once complained. Then, one of her regulars attempted to come to her rescue. The man worked as a clown, as that career was ideal for disguising his horrible features. Indeed, he was always in whiteface with brightly painted red lips, when he visited her. To support himself, he sold helium filled balloons to children and that kept him busy for there were always festivals in one town or another. The balloons were printed with the slogan, "Shop at Wal-Mart, Merida," as they were leftovers from a big promotion at the store and they had been bought by the man for less than half price. Anyway, he tied one of his largest balloons to each of her nipples in an attempt to give her breasts enough aerification to allow her to walk down the hallway to the kitchen where the girls took their meals. The balloons did lift her breasts and held them up, but the strings were in the way as she sat at the dining table. So the solution wasn't perfect. And the balloons would begin to loose their gaseity every few days. That wasn't a serious problem for the man visited her twice a week and brought new balloons each time. By the end of the year she was using three balloons per breast to achieve their aerification and everyone knew—although to spare her feelings no one mentioned it—that her breasts would soon be of a size to outweigh the ability of the balloons to perform their lofty task.

The years passed and her size increased to such a degree that even getting in and out of bed was difficult as the weight of her breasts held her flat. When she overcame the inertia and sat up, her breasts caused her to fall forward. It became easier to just remain in bed. Her noontime customers and her dinnertime customers never failed to bring food and drink for her so she didn't have to make the difficult trip down the hallway to the kitchen. In fact, she decided to no longer even try to get out of bed. She made enough money to employ a maid who kept the room neat and who bathed her, emptied her bed pan, and otherwise tended to her.

Since she didn't leave the brothel, her younger sister, Inez, now came once a week to pick up money for her family. Inez was fourteen years old and much prettier than her older sister and the *putanero* had spotted her—and had an interest in her. Inez would linger in the front parlor, talking to the girls who were waiting there, learning about things she shouldn't yet know, before skipping on home. To tease Inez, a man might reach over and fondle one of the whores. This embarrassed Inez and that made the men laugh. Later, when Inez became sixteen, the *putanero* offered her employment, but only on the condition that Carmelita first agree, for Carmelita was worth more than five or six whores and he didn't want to offend her. Carmelita did agree—but on one condition—and that was that only handsome men be allowed to go to Inez's room. Inez was pretty enough to service only handsome men but the *putanero* feared—rightly, as it turned out—that if a girl went only with handsome men her breasts would diminish in size.

Since Inez was now busy, Josefina, who was fifteen and the next younger sister, now came to the brothel to collect Carmelita's money. Josefina was even prettier than Inez—a fact that was not lost on the *putanero* who made sure there was ice cream and cookies for her when she came on her weekly visits.

By the tenth year Carmelita's breasts were so grossly huge that it was common for a breast to slide off the side of her small bed. When that started to happen she had to quickly push her other breast off the opposite side of the bed to act as a counter weight which would prevent the first breast from dragging her off the bed with it. Once her breasts were on the floor, they were too heavy for the maid to lift them back up. A man was required to come in and lift them. Obviously a much larger bed was needed, and when it was delivered it took four men to lift her out of the old bed and place her on her back in the new one. It had a lovely hand-carved headboard and a Beautyrest mattress.

Her immobility didn't diminish her spirits. Her family was well taken care of. She had so many customers she was never alone and therefore not lonely. She knew the men loved to lie on her pillows of flesh while they made use of her vagina. Yet there was some danger for them. One customer—a thin man—managed to get his head stuck under her left breast and he smothered before he could be pulled out. This was a sad day for Carmelita, especially since she was unable to get out of bed to attend his funeral.

A newspaper reported the man's unusual death and many curiosity seekers came by the brothel. Since a fair number of the curiosity seekers decided to give the girls a try, the girls felt Carmelita could be used to bring customers to the brothel, as that would increase all their fortunes. They elected one girl, Isidora, to bring this insight to the *putanero*.

"What do you want, someone to die every week?" the *putanero* asked her.

"Well, we hadn't thought of that." Isidora replied.

Time passed. Besides Carmelita, Inez and Josefina, their three younger sisters were also now working at the brothel. When Carmelita's mother died suddenly, there was no need—or no place—to send the money. Carmelita decided to donate it to a local church. The padre, wise to the *putanero's* methods of recruitment, sent a boy to collect the money each week.

Oh yes, one last thing: the *putanero* brought back the carpenter once again—for the *putanero* was a man who was never stingy in his appreciation. This time the carpenter enlarged the small window in Carmelita's room so she could enjoy watching the many birds that sang in a nearby tamarindo tree. As everyone knows, birds are particularly found of tamarindo trees.

THE CEMENT FACTORIES

❦

Where to start? It's not enough to say she was beautiful—she was far more than that—she was *una guera magnifica*. A blonde with perfect breasts and legs. Yes, there are Mexican women with perfect breasts and legs. I'm not unsympathetic to their beauty—but they aren't *gueras*, are they? Melanin. Yes, what it comes down to is melanin. Or, perhaps I should say, the lack of it? Melanin so sparse that what we see is the color of the hair fiber itself—that pale blond color that stirs us so. Strange, isn't it? It's what blondes lack—not what they possess—that makes them the rarest of women. It didn't hurt that this particular *guera* had an ass that looked like it had been sculpted by Miguel Norena. This particular *guera* was a rich man's second wife. To use an equine metaphor, she was meant for riding, not breeding. I'm sure you've seen women like her before? Yes, of course, I don't mean close up. Not many of us have had that pleasure. But you get the picture.

The hotel was the most luxurious of the hotels along the *Paseo de Montejo*—at least what passed for luxury in that decade. When the manager was informed she had arrived, he came out to welcome her personally. After small talk about her flight to Merida and the weather—I know she found men like the manager to be hopelessly boring—he concluded with, "Senora H—, if there is anything I can do for you, I hope you will call me personally?"

Everything about her trip had been orderly. The flight had been on time. Taxis weren't air-conditioned in those days but with the windows down she felt comfortable. When she checked in, the clerk had been fawning. Later, this was after she had time to stop and reflect, she was to remember that when she entered the lobby every man had stopped to look at her. That wasn't unusual—men couldn't keep their eyes off her—leering is just another way we men can be boring.

The hotel lobby had been built with a dark magenta marble—it came from *Sierra del Sarnose*, I think; as you know there are no suitable marble quarries in the Yucatan. The hotel has since been demolished to make way for a newer one. It saddens me to think of all that marble being crushed by a wrecker's ball. It's only after we've grown old that such things bother us, isn't it? Anyway, the marble almost exactly matched the manager's skin color. She told him, "I am sure I'll be comfortable here." She had been tempted to say, did you yourself choose the marble? But she told herself to be nice for once.

Her luggage had come in with a porter and the manager snapped his fingers and a bellboy appeared with the room key. "Jorge, please show Senora H— to penthouse B." The conversation had taken place in English, a requisite language for the hotel, then as now.

She followed the bellboy to the elevator. She was wearing a tan linen suit which was narrow at the waist in that European cut designers liked that year, a peach colored silk blouse and high heels. The only jewelry she wore was a wedding band. As she walked, her shoulder length blond hair floated as if she were in slow motion. The bellboy noticed she had green eyes.

The bellboy was shorter than she was—by five or six inches—but then most Mexican men would have been. The bellboy was as dark skinned as the manager but he had the brown skin of an Indian. He could have been thirty or forty. There was a roughness to him—perhaps hardness would be a better word—just under the polished veneer he affected at the hotel. Women found him handsome.

He pressed the button and the door to the elevator opened. He followed her inside and pushed the button for the top floor.

"Are you traveling alone, Senora?" he said.

"Yes. I came to see Chichen Itza," she replied.

"Most Americans come here for the ruins."

"Will you be able to hire a driver for me?"

"Today, Senora?"

"No, for tomorrow."

"Of course."

She looked at him for the first time. "Your name is Jorge, do I remember that right?"

"Yes, Senora."

"Are you part Maya, Jorge?"

"Yes, most Yucatecos are."

"Your English is very good."

"I lived in Texas."

"Doing what?"

"This and that. Have you been to Mexico before, Senora?"

"No. But I make one trip like this every year."

"Ah?"

She felt obligated to finish the conversation. "Last year I went to the Galapagos Islands."

"Where they have the giant turtles?"

"The islands have many interesting creatures."

"Did you go by boat, Senora?"

"Yes, it was wonderful. We took a week just to get there."

"And you went there alone as well?"

"My friends have no interest in third world countries." She hoped that mild insult would end the conversation.

"And your husband?"

"He's too busy. He never takes a vacation."

"Do you have his permission to travel alone?"

"Permission? I wouldn't describe it that way."

"I must say I would not allow my wife to travel so far alone—if she was as blond and beautiful as you are."

"That's a bit impertinent, don't you think?"

"Excuse me, Senora, when we were in the lobby I noticed you have a run in your hose."

Without bothering to look down, she said, "You're certainly observant."

"Perhaps it happened when you kissed your husband goodbye?"

"I doubt that."

"Did the taxi driver get personal?"

She laughed. "What a silly man you are."

They arrived at her floor. He opened the door to the suite and handed her the key, which was warm and sweaty from his hand, and the sensation of touching it startled her.

The suite had a large sitting room furnished with chintz-covered furniture and Chippendale style tables. All the better suites were designed in the English taste as Mexican furniture was still considered too vulgar for rich foreigners. There were fresh flowers on the tables. She walked to the window to view the skyline of the city. At that time, from that height, it would have been possible to see the towers and dome of the cathedral, and the trees in the main plaza. Today there are too many new buildings in the way.

"Should I explain the operation of the TV and the air-conditioning, Senora?"

"I should be capable without you, don't you think?"

"Yes, of course." He carried her luggage into the bedroom.

"Will you summon a maid to unpack for me?" she asked, following him into the room.

"Allow me to unpack for you," he replied.

"Very well, but I'm going to watch you. I don't want you pawing my lingerie."

"Allow me to find a fresh pair of hose for you."

"A beige pair, please, Jorge."

She lit a cigarette and took a seat in an armchair while Jorge carefully hung the contents of two suitcases in the closet. He lined up her shoes in a neat row.

Next, he went to the bathroom with her case of cosmetics and toiletries. She watched him through the open door. When he came back into the bedroom he said, "There were no condoms. Do you wish me to obtain a pack for you?"

"No I don't! That's insulting."

"Mexican men refuse to use them."

"What are you implying?"

"Nothing, Senora."

He carried her last case—which contained her lingerie—to a mahogany chest. He knelt on the floor in front of it and carefully placed her bras in one drawer. Her placed her hose in another, but kept a beige pair to give to her. When he came to her panties he held each pair up to examine it.

"What is this style called? Your panties are so small."

"Bikinis."

"They are so transparent. Are they silk?"

"Why are you so rude?"

"Do you always wear white or do you have any that are black?"

"Why are you so insolent? I only wear white." She crossed her legs nervously.

"They are lovely, nonetheless."

"Am I supposed to say thank-you?"

The next pair he picked up he brought up to his face and breathed in deeply.

"That's enough of that!" she said.

"They have a musky scent that washing has been unable to remove."

"I should report you."

"Do you do your own laundry?"

"Of course not."

"I was wondering, is your pubic hair as blond as the hair on your head?"

"You really are impertinent!"

"Forgive me, but your panties are so transparent I couldn't help but wonder."

"If you must know, yes, I'm blond down there."

"I used to work in a cement factory. It's hard work although the pay is better than most places. But there is nothing much to do in the towns near the factories so the men drink their wages away."

"How fascinating."

He closed the panty drawer, then placed the empty luggage in the closet. He walked over to where she was sitting in the chair and handed her the fresh hose. "Do you wish me to put them on for you, Senora?"

"Do you expect me to let you?"

"Senora, if I had a blond woman working for me—more importantly, a woman who also has blond pubic hair—the men in the cement factories would line up to spend their money with us."

"What are you getting at? What kind of working?"

"Whoring, Senora."

"You're making a joke, right? Is this a quaint national characteristic I haven't heard about?"

"A joke, Senora? No, I am very serious."

"You want *me* to whore for you at a cement factory?"

"Yes."

"Don't be ridiculous!"

"But not at just a factory. No, there are many factories. We could spend a few weeks at each one."

"And I thought you only wanted to change my hose!"

"You would be very popular."

"So, you really are a pimp?"

"No, but I have ambitions."

"And your ambitions now include *me*?"

"Yes."

"Should I be flattered? What about all the local girls, Jorge? You're handsome enough to have a following."

"They don't have blond pubic hair." That remark made her cross her legs again.

"You really are serious, aren't you?"

"When we arrive at each factory I will take you inside so the men can admire you."

"Admire me? And just what would I be wearing?"

"You will need to wear revealing clothes, certainly."

"I can just imagine!"

"There is a maid at the hotel who was a whore before she grew too old. We could exchange your clothes for some of the ones she wore."

She laughed. "My husband hasn't received the bills for all of them yet."

"The maid is smaller than you, which will make her clothes all the more revealing."

"Are there women working at those factories?"

"No. The work is too hard."

"So, it would be just me, paraded in front of all those men while I'm wearing revealing clothes?"

"Yes?"

"And how would you introduce me? Do I get to choose a made-up name? An 'escort' name?"

"It would be easier if I just called you 'my whore.'"

"I don't even get a name? Not, Tiffany? Or, Candy? What are the Mexican equivalents of those names?"

"A name will be unnecessary. I will say, 'my whore will be waiting in her tent.'"

"What tent?"

"Your tent, Senora. The factories are not always near a town."

"You want me to work in a tent?"

"It will be practical for us. We can pitch it along the roadside near the factory."

"How could you get a bed into a tent?"

"A cot, Senora. You will work on a folding cot."

"Let me see if I understand you? You want me to go with you to a cement factory where you'll parade me in front of all the employees."

"Yes."

"And you'll inform them I have, what, a blond pussy?" The tone of her voice had changed from sarcasm to anger.

"Of course."

"Why not let them have a feel or two? At no charge."

"That would certainly encourage them. Yes, I agree to that."

"You also intend to inform them that I'll be waiting to service them in a nearby tent? Lying on my back on a cot? Do I have it straight?"

"Yes, Senora. You understand perfectly."

"Jesus, you're unbelievable! I need another cigarette." She took one from her pack and he moved quickly to light it. "Just for the sake of argument, Jorge, would a whore who works for you have the right to reject a man?"

"Why would you want to do that, Senora?"

"They're rough, dirty men, are they not? Some may be worse?"

"They are hard-working men. Men with few pleasures."

"Surely, you would have some rules, right? Like how many men in one day? Things like that?"

When he didn't answer, she continued, "Why are you being so difficult? Alright, granted, they're all hard-working men. But where would you be while I'm working?"

"In the cab of my truck, next to the tent."

"I suppose you would want me to negotiate what services I would provide?"

"You will provide all services, Senora."

"No restrictions?"

"Men don't like whores who aren't compliant."

"We can put a sign on the outside of the tent—'compliant whore inside.'"

"There will be no need for a sign, Senora. I will tell them you are compliant."

"Jorge, you are really frightening me. I feel faint."

"It is because this is so new to you. Take a couple of deep breaths."

She closed her eyes and took two deep breaths while he went into the bathroom and returned with a glass of water.

"Do you feel better?" he asked.

"I think so." He handed her the glass and she took a drink. "If I let you change my hose will you forget all this silliness?"

She pulled her skirt up to where her garters were exposed. Her legs were as long and sleek as he had imagined them to be. When he got down on his knees between her legs she kicked off her shoes. He unsnapped her hose and rolled them slowly down her legs. She handed him the fresh pair. "Be careful not to run them," she said. Saying that gave her a sense of being in charge. She pointed her toes, making it easier for him to slide on the new pair. He smoothed away any wrinkles by running his hands up her legs, from her ankles to her thighs, then he attached the hose to the garters. He hadn't lingered—as she had expected him to. He had performed the operation without any display of emotion or pleasure.

"How do I know you truly have blond pubic hair?" he said. He was still on his knees between her legs. "I have only your word on it."

She slid her skirt up higher. "There!"

"Yes, you are quite blond, Senora." She lowered her skirt and he stood up. "Now I realize why you wear transparent white panties."

"That's not why I wear them!"

"They reveal your beauty."

"I'd like to go back an hour in time. Request a different bellboy."

"Would you go back in time, Senora?"

"Yes, I just said I would!"

"I think you are actually very brave. This must be difficult for you. Yet, I know you find my offer exciting."

"Do you actually expect me to become your whore?"

"I think you want to."

"Don't be silly." She was silent for a moment. "Jorge, what do you think my services would be worth? I mean, it's only a theoretical question. Every woman must wonder what she would be worth?"

"It depends on what is asked of you."

"What do Mexican men like?"

"Your customers will be so eager to get between your legs—pardon the expression, Senora—I doubt if they will stop to consider any unusual requests. If they do, I will price them fairly."

"Still, you haven't told me how much my services would be?"

"For a man to lie between you legs, Senora, 200 pesos."

"Jorge, that's twenty dollars?"

"Mexico is a poor country. For you to get on your knees in front of a man, 100 pesos."

"Ten dollars?"

"The tent will offer no amenities—except for you."

"But really, Jorge, ten dollars?"

"Have you been on your knees for a man, Senora?"

"Yes, of course, I'm not a prude."

"Did you charge him?"

"Certainly not!"

"So you have done it many times at no charge?"

"Are you hard of hearing? I've never charged anyone."

"I'm simply saying the 100 pesos you earn on your knees is 100 pesos more than you have ever gotten."

She laughed. "That's one way of looking at it."

"And for a man to use your ass—"

"Please don't even suggest that!"

"Senora, there will be men who will want your ass. You will charge 250 pesos for that pleasure."

"Oh God!"

"Senora—"

"What if someone wanted to do all three things! Do I offer a discount!"

"Ah? The three should be 550 pesos. But it would be unfair to turn a man down because he lacks a few pesos? Don't you agree?"

"Jorge, please stop saying things like, 'you will do this and you will do that.' I haven't agreed to anything. Nor do I intend to."

"But I think you are ready to say yes, Senora."

"Is that what you think?"

"I know women, Senora."

"You don't know me." She looked at him defiantly.

"No?" he said calmly. "There is a very fine brothel not far from here where the women are expensive. But you wouldn't want to work there, would you?"

"Of course I wouldn't!"

"If I had suggested working there you would have thrown me out of the room?"

"Of course I would have!"

"But when I suggested working out of a tent, earning 100 pesos on your knees—that didn't get me thrown out?"

"I could still do it."

"When I said you would be required to be 'compliant,' I'm sure I saw your eyes light up."

"You're mistaken. My eyes were just tearing. Why would I want to be 'compliant?'"

"Because it seems exciting to you, Senora."

"Really? You should be a psychiatrist—not a pimp."

"I want to be your pimp."

"You're not going to be."

"I liked the way you suggested letting the men feel you up."

"But I was being sarcastic; I was ridiculing your plans."

"Were you?"

"Don't you understand sarcasm?"

"Let's just see, shall we?"

"What do you mean?"

"Do you think you should wear clothes while you are waiting for customers in your tent? Lying there with your legs spread apart so your blond pubic hair is the first thing a man sees."

"That sounds filthy."

"Filthy? Perhaps, but also exciting?"

"Of course not . . ."

"Think about my question, Senora."

She thought for a moment. Finally she said, "Wait, before I answer your question, I have one for you. Have you ever done this to any other guests?"

"No, Senora."

"I mean, if you had, I would want to talk to them."

"To see how it turned out?"

"Do you blame me?"

"There are no others."

"But, Jorge, isn't what you want me to do illegal? I mean, what about the police?" There was desperation in her voice.

"The police will be among your customers."

"But I don't even speak Spanish!"

"Si is the only word you will need to know."

"Oh, yes, I forgot, I'm to be compliant!"

"I'm waiting for your answer."

"I can't believe this!" She ran her fingers nervously through her hair.

"Senora—"

"It would be a waste of time, taking my clothes on and off." Her voice was very soft and she was unable to look him in the eye.

"So, that is your recommendation? To leave them off?"

"Yes." She let the glass she was holding fall to the floor, spilling what water was left in it.

"Where is your sarcasm?"

"Just how long do you expect me to do this?"

"There are factories in the Yucatan, Quintana Roo, Chipas, Campeche, Tabasco. It would take years to do them all even if you were to work only a few weeks at each one."

"Years? You must be kidding? I'll do it for a couple of months. I want to have the experience—have a little fun—not have a career."

"Senora, by 'couple' do you mean 'two?'"

"Well . . . yes, I suppose so." She sighed. "I feel better now—I shouldn't, but I do—you really frightened me when you first brought up this subject, do you know that?"

"Because you knew you would say yes?"

"No! I had no intention of saying yes."

"But since you are no longer frightened, you can say yes to more time?"

"But, Jorge, I'm just doing this on a lark."

"Do you think I will give up my job so you can have fun for a couple of months?"

"Well, I . . ."

"Do you think the hotel will rehire me after I leave with a guest?"

"If I ask them to take you back?"

"They don't allow whores in the hotel lobby."

"Please don't use that term when referring to me."

"You would be unable to help me."

"Are jobs like yours hard to come by?"

"Very."

"And you would be out of work?"

"Yes."

"Perhaps I am being unreasonable?" She thought for a moment. "How many ruins are there around here? Enough to convince my husband it took months to see them all?"

"There are hundreds of ruins."

"I mean, I want to do it. But I don't know about more time?"

"There may be a thousand ruins."

"Alright, I will do it for ONE year. He'll buy that. Jesus, did I just say a year? I can't believe I just said a year! OK, but no more—remember, I have obligations, a life to lead back in New York."

"Of course. But you're young?"

"I'm twenty-six."

"Then you could give me ten years, easily, then go back to your other obligations."

"Ten years? That's impossible. One year and no more."

He picked up the empty glass and carried it back to the bathroom. When he returned he said, "Ten years would be better."

"Jorge, please be reasonable."

"We should plan to leave the hotel in a few hours."

"Should I pack?" She laughed nervously. "You just unpacked for me!"

"Your clothes are going to belong to the maid."

"I thought perhaps you were joking about that?"

"You will have no need for clothes like the ones you brought with you."

"No? Surely we will take a break once in a while? What do you do for fun, Jorge? You must do something?"

"I should call the maid." He picked up the phone and dialed it. Someone answered and he spoke rapidly in Spanish, which she couldn't understand. When he hung up he said, "She was very surprised but delighted to have this opportunity. She wishes to apologize for the poor condition of her clothes, but promises she will pick out her sexiest items. She will bring them here shortly."

"I don't think I want to meet her."

"You could ask her for some professional advice."

"No."

"She knows things—"

"I don't care. I can figure them out for myself."

"We still need to resolve the amount of time you are willing to work."

"But I said one year?"

"And I said ten."

"Jorge, let's make it one year, OK?"

"What if I said I wouldn't take you for only one year?"

"Oh?"

"Would you like me to just walk away, Senora?"

"No."

"You could see Chichen Itza then return to New York?"

"You know I don't want that now . . ."

"Senora, have you looked closely at your pubic hair?"

"What?"

"You have a few dark hairs. Please spread your legs."

She spread her legs.

"Wider."

"Like this?" To spread her legs wider she was forced to rest them over the arms of the chair. "This is embarrassing," she said.

He pulled the crotch of her panties aside. "I noticed them earlier."

"I didn't know. I mean, how often do I look at myself?"

He let the panties slip back in place, then removed his fingers. "When you spread your legs it should look like the sun is rising."

"And a few dark hairs spoil that?"

"What would you consider to be your greatest asset, Senora?"

"I know you want me to say my blond pussy!" She slid her legs off the arms of the chair.

"Then say it."

"My intellect is my greatest asset."

"No, it's your blond pussy."

"What if it is!" she snapped.

"Then you should give it your most loving care, Senora."

"Like do something about the dark hairs?" She looked down. "I don't see that many?"

"One would be too many."

"I suppose I can bleach them? Get some peroxide?"

"I want you to use it every week, Senora."

"I've never used peroxide before but I doubt if I'll need it every week? If I do, I'll do it. It's difficult for me to understand how important my pubic hair is." When he didn't respond she said, "You can inspect me until you're satisfied I've gotten it right."

"I'll inspect you every week, Senora. Now, we still need to resolve the amount of time you are willing to work."

"Jorge, you're going to make a lot of money, aren't you? Or should I say, we are?"

"By Mexican standards, a lot of money."

"I don't care how much, really. I've never earned any money in my life. This won't mean anything to you but at school we were contemptuous of earning money except through intellectual pursuits. You are going to have a highly educated whore working for you."

"When you are on your knees, Senora, remind your customer of your education."

"Don't get me wrong, I'm intrigued by this. I mean, the tent is deliciously tacky. But for one year, OK? A year is a long time but it would still be like doing something on a lark. Any longer would be like having a genuine, unrefuted career. I mean, it's an arbitrary distinction. Still, it's a distinction I want to make. One year it's a lark. Longer it's a career." She had what she felt was a brilliant idea—the hotel manager would take her side! "The manager said to call him if I needed anything. Will you accept him as a mediator?"

"He doesn't like me."

"So much the better. If he says one year, will you accept that?"

"Yes."

She sat on the bed and dialed the manager's number. "Senor, this is Sandra H—."

"Ah, Senora, how do you find your suite?"

"The suite is lovely but Jorge and I are having a disagreement—"

"Jorge? Our bellboy?"

"Yes. I'm going to take you up on your kind offer and ask you to come up and mediate our disagreement."

"Senora, I apologize for any misunderstanding between you and any of our employees. They are not allowed to have a disagreement with you. I'll be up immediately."

She turned to Jorge and said, "He's on his way."

"Senora, please remove your clothes."

"Jorge, I said the manager is on his way!"

"If you are dressed, the manager will not take you seriously. He will think we are—what is the American expression?—pulling his leg."

"Jorge, please don't do this to me! Let me wear my bra and panties. And my hose—you went to all that trouble?"

"Senora—".

"Am I supposed to do whatever you want? Is that the correct whore/pimp relationship?" She removed her jacket and laid it on the bed. She unbuttoned her blouse and folded it on top of her jacket. Her pale nipples were visible through the thin material of her bra. She slid her skirt down her legs and stepped out of it and left it on the floor. She looked down at her panties. How could my bush be so important, she wondered. I could have an IQ of 60 and no one would care.

There was a knock on the door and they went back into the sitting room.

She opened the door and when the manager came in he said, "Senora, you aren't wearing a dress?"

"I'm getting a new wardrobe, so to speak," she answered.

"Yet—"

"My wardrobe isn't what I need your help with. I'm going to be leaving today."

"You don't like the hotel?"

"Of course I like it. But I'm going with Jorge—"

"With Jorge? The bellboy?" The manager came into the room and closed the door behind him,

"I'm going to work with—for him."

"Doing what, Senora?"

"Well, I suppose you must know. I'm going to be a prostitute for a year."

"Jorge is a pimp?" The manager was looking at Jorge but he had asked her the question.

"He is now."

"Did you come here with this in mind?"

"Certainly not!" she snapped. "This is as incomprehensible to me as it must be to you. But what I—we—need your help with is that I have agreed to work for one year and Jorge wants me to work for ten years. Can we count on you to be a neutral mediator?"

"I assume if I were to fire Jorge immediately you would just leave with him?"

"Yes. But the amount of time I'm to be with him would be unresolved."

He turned to Jorge. "Senora H— was a guest! How could you possibly broach such a subject with a guest?"

"She has blond pubic hair."

"She does?"

"Yes."

"Even so, Jorge, even so . . ."

"Are you going to help us?" she interjected.

He thought for a minute. He wiped his brow with a handkerchief. "Very well, I will do it but only because I want to protect you, Senora."

"You can protect me by convincing Jorge to accept one year."

"I have to sit down," he said. He sat in one of two facing chairs. Jorge sat in the other one. She started to sit on the sofa but Jorge said, "Please remain standing, Senora. It is easier to have a discussion about you if you are standing in front of us."

She remained standing and clasped her hands behind her back, lowering her head as if she were a young girl who had just been scolded.

"Let's start again," the manager said. "Senora, give me your reasons why you feel one year is the right amount of time?"

"I'm still confused as to why I said yes to all this. No, I take that back— it should be a once in a lifetime experience. But I wanted to do it for a couple of months! Jorge's going to have me servicing factory workers on a cot in a tent—that's the reason it's so, well, appealing—the reason I've now agreed to a year. But even that kind of fun will certainly wear thin before a year is up. And if I'm not having fun, what's the point?"

"Now, Jorge, why do you insist on ten years when the Senora clearly knows what will make her happy?"

"Because we will have to travel a great deal. That means I will have to buy a new truck. There are other expenses, such as the tent. And I expect she will wear out the cots, maybe one every month or so—they don't stand up to a lot of hard use. No, I would not get my money back in one year."

The manager cleared his throat. "Yes, I didn't consider your expenses, Jorge."

"And food, Senor. We have to eat three times a day. And medical expenses. I will have to buy salves and balms when she complains of soreness."

"Senora," the manager said, "Jorge does have the better argument."

"He does?"

"Yes. As a neutral mediator, I have to suggest that it would be better if you agree to a longer time."

"But?"

"I'm trying to be fair."

"Like how much longer?"

"Somewhere between your two positions, I should think. Say, five years?"

"Five years? Do you realize what you're asking?"

"But one year simply isn't reasonable. Trucks are expensive in Mexico. He will want one that is air-conditioned—"

"The tent won't be air-conditioned!"

"Still, consider all the other expenses he listed. If you agree to five years I'm sure Jorge will give up his insistence on ten."

"What would prevent me from just leaving no matter what I agree to?"

Jorge spoke with a firmness that surprised her. "Senora, after we agree on a length of time, I will not allow you to leave prematurely."

"Would you tie me up?" she said teasingly.

"Yes. And do more if need be."

"I'm sure the Senora won't need tying up?" the manager stammered.

When Jorge didn't respond, she said, "What does it take to make you laugh?"

"The Maya haven't laughed in 500 years," the manager said. "Since the Spanish came."

"No? Well that's one more reason to do this for just one year."

"But you are at a standoff, Senora, and, in truth, one year doesn't protect Jorge's investment in you."

"You're suggesting I actually agree to five years?"

"That would be meeting Jorge half way, which most would agree is the fair way to do things."

"I can't believe I'm standing here in my underwear having this conversation."

"Five years would be a fair compromise."

"I just came here to see some Mayan cities!"

"But you are going to make love to the descendants of the men who built the cities."

"Ummm, that's an interesting way to look at it . . ."

"Surely that is much better than merely seeing the ruins?"

"They really are the descendants, aren't they?"

"Yes, Senora. Their ancestors were great masons."

"Now they work at cement factories. How consistent."

"Senora, you'll be laboring under the laborers," Jorge said.

"I know you think that kind of talk turns me on."

"Doesn't it?"

"Perhaps. But relative to one year. Not five. Certainly not ten!"

The manager interrupted. "Senora, by now I hope you recognize I have your interests at heart?"

"Yes."

"Then let me pose this question. Could five years be five times more fun than one?"

"And if it isn't?"

Jorge started to walk toward the door. "Senora, I'm going to return to my post downstairs. I can wait for another blond gringa."

"Jorge, wait . . ." she said. "This is difficult . . ."

"Your choice may be between five years and none?" the manager said.

"I know! I know!" Then more calmly, "Were there Mayan prostitutes?"

"Of course. They most likely worked out of a tent, Senora," the manager replied. "Pitched near to where the men were."

She chewed on a fingernail. "I can't believe I'm actually considering five years . . ."

"But you are, Senora?"

"Yes . . ."

"Then do it, Senora, so we can hopefully conclude this and all of us can be on our way."

"Alright! Alright! But *five* years, not ten."

" Jorge, what do you say to that?" the manager said, pleased that he had reached a compromise.

"Even if we stayed only a few weeks at each factory it would take five years just to do the Yucatan, Quintana Roo, and Campeche. What about Chipas and Tobasco?" Jorge said.

"Jorge, that's beside the point," the manager replied. He turned to her. "Yet it is true, I would hate to have you leave Mexico before you got to see Chipas and Tobasco."

"How much am I going to see from the inside of a tent? No, five years is all I can do."

"I still insist on ten years," Jorge replied.

"What?" she screamed.

"Jorge! You are being unreasonable! The Senora met you half way!" There was exasperation in the manager's voice. "Now, I'm going to listen to one more argument from each of you then I, myself, will decide if it is to be five years or ten. Do you both agree that my word is final?"

"Yes," Jorge said.

"Yes," she said.

"Alright, then, Senora, you may go first."

"If I thought there was even a remote chance Jorge could prevail I wouldn't do this. Senor, I have a life back in New York. I have a husband. I have friends. I have a position in the community—I'm involved in charities and there are artists who depend on my patronage. As soon as I said yes to five years I knew I had made a mistake. If I'm ever to return successfully to my former life it will be because I returned sooner rather than later. If I were to stay with Jorge for ten years what would I have to return to? No husband! No friends! Nothing! Surely you understand that?"

"Of course I understand, Senora. Your argument is very persuasive. You have another life—an important one—and you wish to return to it. Now, Jorge, I'm doubtful you can overcome the Senora's most persuasive argument. You can concede now if you wish."

"Stay here while I get something." Jorge went into the bedroom and they could hear a drawer being opened. He returned with one of her panties.

"Are those her undergarments?" the manager asked.

"Put them up to your face and breathe in," Jorge said, handing them to the manager.

The manager was uncertain if he should do it, yet he cautiously placed her panties over his face and took a deep breath. "Very musky, indeed," he said. He took a second deep breath then a third and a fourth and a fifth. This went on for a while.

"What kind of argument is that?" she asked.

"Under normal circumstances, an argument that would have little merit," the manager said. "But these are not normal circumstances, are they? I placed your panties over my face as Jorge requested, Senora, and I realized his argument—although made without words—was truly sublime. We Mexicans understand metaphysical reasoning. I suddenly understood that you, shall I say, belong in Mexico. As a North American, you may wonder how his argument, using only your panties, could be more persuasive to me than your understandable and reasonable desire to get back to your life in America."

"You mean it is?"

"Yes, certainly. I rule that ten years will be the length of time you work for Jorge."

"Oh, my God!" she said.

"Sit down, Senora," the manager said in his kindest voice. "It must have been very tiring standing there."

She collapsed on the sofa in a very unladylike pose with her legs splayed. There was a look of disbelief on her face. But, at the same time, she had never looked lovelier in all her twenty-six years.

The manager turned to speak to Jorge. "She is disappointed but it will be only temporary. Now, I hope you will accept some advice from an older man? The Senora could become bored. If she becomes bored she may try to manipulate you—or even run away. My advice is to keep her busy day and night. Do the factories pay the men monthly or weekly?"

"Weekly."

"That will help your traffic flow. But reduce her prices rather than let her be idle. If no one has more than fifty pesos, then fifty pesos becomes her price. Keep magazines in the tent, magazines that depict a variety of unusual sex acts—in the hope they will inspire her customers. All this will insure she doesn't become bored."

The manager turned to the Senora who, having overheard the conversation, sat up.

"A variety of unusual sex acts?" she said.

"Senora, I hope my frankness was not upsetting?" the manager replied.

"That terrifies me!"

"Oh? Well, I'm sure Jorge will forget about the magazines if you ask him."

"I don't want to become bored . . ."

"Of course not."

"What kind of magazines?"

"The German ones are the best."

"No, I mean what would they depict?"

"Solutions to your potential boredom, Senora."

Now in tears, she turned to Jorge. "Please, Jorge, can I go back to one year? You won't be sorry! I'll work so hard you'll get all your money back—and more!" When he didn't respond she lay back on the sofa in a fetal position.

"When you agreed to five years I knew you were an exceptional woman," the manager said. "A woman capable of . . . Even so, I was prepared to rule in your favor when you made your argument."

Her tears stopped. "Jorge was too clever."

"Too Mexican, Senora," the manager said.

"Yes, too something."

Jorge put his hand on her shoulder. "I want you to send a letter to your husband."

"Please, no . . . if I do that he'll divorce me."

"Do you expect him to wait ten years?" he replied.

"No . . . but . . ."

"Tell him what you are going to be doing for 250 pesos."

"Jorge, I can't say that!"

"Oh? Is it something he may have wanted from you but didn't get?"

"No, of course not! The subject never came up." She stood. "Let's make a deal, OK? If I don't have to write the letter I promise never to complain when someone wants that . . ."

"You'll find stationery in the desk."

The manager, disturbed by the tone of the conversation, attempted to change the subject. "Do you speak Spanish, Senora?" It was all he could think to say.

"What's the Spanish word for compliant?" she replied. She went to the desk and found the stationery.

"Sumiso?"

"I know two words. Si and sumiso." She laughed, " No, make that three. Add peroxido." She found a pen in the drawer.

The manager continued. "If you will permit, Senora, I will have a bottle of champagne brought up. I want to make a toast!"

"Damn it, I can't find any stamps!" she said.

After the champagne was brought up and opened, Senora H—, Jorge, the manager, and the maid—who had arrived with a suitcase— polished off the bottle quickly. The manager made many toasts. The maid tried on all her new clothes and danced around like a child on Christmas day.

When the manager and the maid left the suite, the Senora phoned the front desk. That's where I come in and why I am able to tell her story.

I was a management trainee at that hotel, merely eighteen years old. I was the one who answered the phone that afternoon—I recognized her voice immediately. She was requesting that someone run out to a pharmacy. I had fallen in love with her when I saw her arrive at the hotel so I was eager to help. I volunteered to run the errand.

"What type of peroxide?" I asked, not knowing if there were different types.

"I'm afraid I don't know," she said. "Better pick up some ammonia as well."

"If you tell me what you want to use if for I will ask the pharmacist," I replied.

She told me and I'm not ashamed to say I was unable to bring myself to speak to anyone at the pharmacy. I grabbed the first bottles I found on the shelf.

When I delivered the bleaching agents to the suite she answered the door. She was in her underwear but she invited me inside. That's when I saw Jorge. I didn't recognize him at first, since he had changed out of his uniform into street clothes. "She needs help with the peroxide," he said. I was too stunned to say no.

I followed her into the bathroom where she casually removed her panties. Her back was to me. When she turned to face me I was dumbfounded. How can I describe what she possessed between her legs? It was like the sun, just as it rises above the horizon, momentarily blinding you. Unaware of how dumbfounded I was, she sat on the toilet seat and calmly gave me instructions. When she lit a cigarette smoke blew across my face.

Now on my knees, I separated the dark hairs from the blond ones by tying them together with small bows I made from Kleenex tissue. This took an hour—longer than it might, for my hands trembled like a man with palsy. I stood back. I had created a field of small bows— a small work of art. I never visit museums. Do you know why? Because I suffer when I look at treasures I know I can't possess. That's how I felt at that moment. Blinded. Dumbfounded. Suffering. Nevertheless, I persevered. Using a bathroom drinking glass I mixed a small amount of ammonia into the peroxide. I was startled when it began to foam and she laughed. The solution was easy to apply with a cotton ball—but it was caustic. I was determined not let it touch her flesh. Of course my hands received burns. Better they burn to the elbows' than a drop of that liquid touch her. My hands were expendable. I was afraid that if I left to find a pair of gloves she might decide she no longer needed my help.

As I worked she chain-smoked and began talking. In a remarkably calm way she told me how she had come to agree to work for Jorge for ten years. "Do you think he'll let me go after a year or two?" she asked.

When the darker hairs had lightened to where they would blend in with the others, I took a wash cloth with warm water and carefully washed her. I dried her with a towel. Then I took a comb from my pocket and arranged her hair until it had a symmetry that pleased me. The entire procedure took two hours—perhaps a little longer—but I would have been willing to stay there, on my knees, until hell froze over.

Jorge joined us in the bathroom. When he ran his fingers brusquely through her hair I decided I hated him. But he was pleased with the results. "We're going up to Telchac," he said. "Visit her whenever you want."

Every Wednesday, my day off, I went to wherever it was they had pitched their tent, as they moved from town to town. I didn't have a car in those days so I would take a bus from Merida and then walk, sometimes miles along dusty roads, wearing my business suit as I hoped this gentility would appeal to her.

I was overweight in those days—I liked to say it was just baby fat—and there was little room for the two of us on her cot. Lord, how that cot shook! But it wasn't the likes of management trainees that she wanted. She tolerated me because I had paid 200 pesos for her. No, she wanted those unwashed buggers who waited their turn outside the tent—as many as twenty of them at a time waiting, stoically, no matter how fiercely the sun beat down on them.

At the end of the summer my father died and I was summoned back to the capitol to take over the family business. I made one last visit to their tent and after I had finished and dressed, I told her I was leaving. She got up, came over to me, and without saying a word kissed me on the lips.

It has been, what, thirty years since the day I answered the phone call from her suite? There hasn't been a day that's passed that I haven't paused to think about her, a night when she hasn't entered my dreams.

Now, I am determined to find her.

Recapture a part of my youth? Well, why not? I know, that sounds commonplace. Yet, why should it? What man doesn't want to recapture a little of his youth? I want to get down on my knees again and be as blinded as I was before. I want to be on my knees while she sits in front of me—her legs spread wide as a church door—so I may perform the same pharmacology, no, let's call it the same alchemy: for I'll be turning what's common into gold. I'll leave my gloves at home as the burns from the peroxide and ammonia will be my proof that a man is capable of living both in the past and in the present.

Yes, of course, my chances of finding her are poor. Yet, who knows? I felt it was likely she had returned to New York, where she would surely be out of my reach, but she has not. Through connections at our embassy, enquiries were made. To my surprise, I learned that her husband was still living and was willing to discuss her. In a letter to me he stated his belief that she never returned to the States. In any case, he heard no more from her after receiving the letter Jorge insisted she write.

Do you see that enormous pile of phone books? Even in a den as cluttered as mine, an eight foot pile of books must stand out? Yes, my old friend, I knew you would be too polite to ask about them—although they must have intrigued you? They cover the Yucatan, Quintana Roo, Campeche, Tabasco, Chiapas, Veracruz, Oaxaca, and every other state in the Republic.

I have been calling pharmacies in each of the towns.

"Do you have a blond gringa who regularly buys peroxide from you?" I ask.

This has gone on for weeks with no one responding yes. As you might imagine, there are thousands of pharmacies in thousands of towns. I realize he could have taken her anywhere. They could be in the gold fields of Brazil, for all I know—a thousand miles into the jungle— where men bargain for what they want with nuggets the size of a fist and blondes are as rare as snow.

Yet I'm not discouraged. I've ordered phone books from Brazil— along with all the other countries on the continent. I expect their arrival any day.

CONSUELA AND HER PUSSY THAT CAN SEE INTO THE FUTURE

꧁

No one knows who discovered it—the exceptional faculty that Consuela's pussy has—for almost every man in town now claims he was the one. Since this discovery took place some years ago, and the debate among the claimants has gone unresolved, how likely is it we will ever know? Still, this isn't an idle debate, by no means, for it turns out her pussy is an oracle. Many of the men who listened to it have become rich beyond their dreams. Let me make one thing clear—her pussy isn't an oracle like the ones found in ancient Greece. Those mediums spoke in parables, whereas her pussy is straightforward and candid. It wants everyone who listens to it to gain knowledge and, hopefully, immediate riches. Her pussy actually told one man which candidate would be elected president of Mexico. Unfortunately, Consuela can't hear it speak for she is deaf in one ear and that impediment means she, herself, will likely remain poor.

The fact that her pussy might have a purpose beyond providing pleasure for the local populace and a few traveling salesmen seemed unlikely, and it's therefore understandable why its curiosa felicitas had been so long overlooked by us. We don't get tourists here in Tixholop. If we did, I fear the discovery would surely have gone to one of them? So many foreigners seem to have, shall I say, a taste for a certain debased vice . . . I hope it isn't necessary to tell you that we Mexican men don't have that vice, yet we understand it is common among

Americans and the French. Although it would have likely guaranteed an early discovery, it's a vice that is *indigno de hombre*.

Where had that tiny voice come from? A voice with its perfect Castilian Spanish—which is a dialect Consuela, herself, does not speak. Perhaps it wasn't a voice after all but a breeze rustling the curtains? The men went to the window. But in our town a breeze is no more likely to be stirring than are the thighs underneath our wives' nightgowns. A radio? Consuela didn't even have electricity at her house, let along a radio.

Eventually someone, guessing at the likely source, nestled his ear next to her pussy. Consuela has been unable to remember who that first man was although, in truth, ears were not what most men wanted to nestle down there. Shouldn't that have been memorable to her, you say? The problem is, Consuela has a great many customers and she often-times confuses them. She's usually not able to tell the difference between, say, Rudolfo the butcher and Domingo the carpenter. (Although she remembers that one or the other has a large *pinga*.) And what about the men who had declined to give her their names, or had used false names?

Come to think of it, it was probably Ernesto the bus driver who was first, for shortly after being with her—this was nearly thirty years ago—he ran out and bought Microsoft at . . .

THE BOASTFUL WHORE

What distinguished Valentia from all the other whores was not her beauty—for we are indeed fortunate to have many whores in our town who are beautiful—although, since she resembled Kitty de Hoyo, it's certainly true that she was the most beautiful of them all. No, what distinguished Valentia was her outlandish boasting. It is well known that girls who are beautiful can get away with a lot of annoyingly bad habits.

The men of Tizimin are known for their patience when it comes to beautiful women. For we are in awe of beauty in all its forms. We will put up with petty thievery, a little laziness in a girl's horizontal duties, and modest boasting. What happened to this particular whore didn't need to take place. I have thought about it over the years, and I've come to the conclusion it was the girl's fault. And hers alone. For the men did their best to ignore her unfortunate habit and might have continued doing so forever, had she not started boasting that she could tire out a stallion. Although she made that boast only when she was drunk, the men still grew tired of hearing it, since they sensed it was a reflection on their prowess as much as it was just her opinion of her supposed Olympian abilities.

One morning four men came to her room; they woke her and forced her to dress, then told her she was to be taken out to a hacienda that bred horses. Why would I want to go such a place? she complained. You will like what you find there, they teased. She recognized the men, and given some time she might have remembered their names, for she had been with each of them. Two were caballeros who came into town once in a while, and before today they had always been polite to her, always leaving her with a small tip although she knew caballeros received poor wages.

What is the name of this place? she asked as they led her outside. The sun was just coming up; a sight she hadn't seen in years. Hacienda de Grijalva, they replied. The hacienda was a two-hour trip from Tizimin, and she was forced to ride in the back of an old Ford truck with Basillo, one of the men. The truck stunk for it had been hauling horse manure. That shouldn't bother someone fond of horses, Basillo told her. She searched for a way out of the fix she was in—for she knew she was in a fix—although its exact nature wasn't yet clear to her.

To a pretty whore, seducing her captor must have seemed like the most obvious way out—let Basillo know what could be his if he just became her ally. After all, hadn't everyone always told her that she looked just like that famous movie star? And what man wouldn't have sacrificed every possession he had for Kitty de Hoyo? She slid over to him so she could press the length of her movie star's body against him. He allowed her to kiss him but then he laughed and said, That won't work, and he pushed her away. What could the *bastardo* do anyway, she must have thought. He isn't the driver and I'm not going to jump out of a moving truck!

It was hot and dusty and they passed a few milpa patches where people were working, and a few kilometers of stunted wild flowers, but there was little else to look at, as those of you who have traveled this road know. Basillo didn't like the back of the truck anymore than she did, especially when the truck hit a large bump, but he had been told to watch her. The other three men rode in the cabin, where they had the truck's radio playing American country music in English. Sometimes we receive stations from as far away as Texas.

I'm sure she must have remembered someone saying the hacienda is east of Yasihon? For she had plenty of customers from the hacienda—all the girls did. Because there is so little to do in Yalsihon the caballeros come to Tizimin for their fun. The hacienda has been there for generations—from the days of the first Spanish—and was one of the few that survived intact from the 1910 Revolution. The patron of the time had been clever enough to ally himself with Aquiles Serdan and that crowd. He knew President Diaz would certainly be overthrown.

Anyway, the hacienda is known for breeding horses that race

throughout rural Mexico. But not at the prestige tracks, for de Grijalva horses are considered too wild to race against the pampered thoroughbreds that have come to dominate the big city races. De Grijalva horses were bred to stand up to Maya and Aztec spears without fear, and that temperament has never been bred out of them. They acquitted themselves admirably when Winfield Scott landed in Veracruz in 1847. It was said that had there been more de Grijalva horses and fewer Mexican generals the course of the war could have been reversed. The Yucatan is a hard, dry country and horses that prosper here are usually mean beasts, as hard and unforgiving as the rest of us Yucatacos.

At the hacienda, the whore was led to a small corral. There were men at the gate and they stepped aside to let her in. Inside the corral, she was told to remove her clothes—which she did without protest. One of the men told her to climb up the steps to a wooden platform that had been constructed for her. When she reached the top the men cheered as she stood naked before them. But in the bright light of morning—which is every whore's worst friend—it was clear to us that, although she was still beautiful, she had begun to show the wear and tear inherent to all labourers who exploit their bodies.

Although the platform must have been constructed hastily it was by no means slipshod, for there were steps along the side and the joinery spoke of having been built by one the hacienda's fine carpenters. The fact that it had been constructed in her honor—and with such care—likely gave her little satisfaction. The corral was shaded by large trees—which was a relief—yet, of course, the trees had been planted to shade valuable horses, not boastful whores.

Men had been drifting to the hacienda all morning and by now a large crowd had gathered around the coral. There were also a number of young boys, ten to fifteen or sixteen years old and they pretended nonchalance at her nudity, but they couldn't take their eyes off her. Some of them had erections and kept their hands in their pockets to take advantage of that unexpected pleasure. The boys had come with dogs in tow and when dogs get together fights break out among them and the men had to kick at them to break them up.

The mayor arrived late and was amazed at the size of the crowd. He immediately wondered—could such a thing become an annual event, a source of much needed tourist dollars for Tizimin? I remember speaking to him about this—for I was standing next to him. There were serious questions, of course. Our Festival of the Three Kings, which takes place every November, is well known and we discussed whether or not the priests from the Iglesia Los Tres Reyes would find fault with a competing festival. Also, would the Stallion Festival—as the mayor was already calling it—have the same appeal if the girl were a willing participant? The mayor and I frequently had philosophical discussions about how to blend secular and sacred concerns in this modern world we find ourselves in. The Stallion Festival may have been an impractical idea but a mayor has heavy responsibilities; who can fault him for thinking of his town?

When Valentia was up on the platform she was told to get down on all fours in a thin layer of straw, and that brought her up to just the right height. In that position on the platform, the carpenter had calculated she would be about fourteen hands tall. A blanket from a broodmare was placed over her back so that it left her rear exposed and her sex available. The blanket smelled strongly of horse. She made no attempt to get away; she was sober but she wished she were drunk for she now knew which boast had brought her here. Let me have a drink, she said. Water? the men teased. No, some whisky, she replied. What's your favorite brand, they laughed. We'll have some brought out from Tizimin.

A breeding hobble was placed around her neck, then threaded under her belly, back to her legs, and adjusted to her size. Hock straps were attached to the back of her knees, then secured to the hobble straps. Her left leg had been pulled inward in what is called a Scotch hobble, to prevent her from possibly moving forward. She was rendered immobile, just as a mare wearing the very same hobble had been the day before.

The wagering began. I'm not a betting man but even I was tempted to bet a few pesos. The odds varied considerably, but I don't believe they ever favored her. When all bets were made, a black stallion, excited by the smell from the blanket, was brought bucking and kicking into the small corral.

The stallion quickly mounted her and the weight of his front legs held her tight, as if he didn't trust the way she was hobbled. The men cheered as his enormous member penetrated her. She managed to take its entire length, although with some difficulty. The stallion had enormous stamina—which is why it had won so many races—and the men were suddenly uneasy about what they had done. Some of them made the sign of the cross and swore to go to confession as soon as possible. Seeing the horse's *pinga* move in and out of her at such a dazzling speed had rendered most of us speechless, and there was no more cheering. The mayor's hopes evaporated.

The men had expected the whore to shout oaths at them—oaths that were her appraisals of their manhood. A few of the coarser of them shamelessly called her a *corralera*. But she remained silent with her teeth tightly clenched and her eyes tightly closed. Perhaps she was praying? If so, then God chose to answer the men's prayers, not the whore's.

An hour passed. All the whore had to do was say, "I was wrong, I am only a boastful whore and I cannot tire out a stallion!" and the men would laugh, but they would remove the horse from the corral.

The contest lasted close to another hour. No one was sure how many times a horse could ejaculate for, mounted on a mare, once was considered enough and the horses were separated. How many times was it with the stallion? One man said he thought it had been six times but he had to count on his fingers and one or two of them were missing.

Finally, the whore said, "Stop, the horse is too much for me, I cannot tire it out!" The horse, of course, didn't want to stop but two men entered the pen and managed, with some difficulty, to separate the two unlikely lovers. The black stallion was led away; bets were paid off or collected; and the whore was returned to her room in town.

There may be readers who question the veracity of this tale. I was there but, of course, you may wonder if I am prone to artistic license? No, when I was a schoolboy, over half a century ago, my professors told me I was without imagination—and I have done little since to disprove them. They steered me toward law, as opposed to, say, *belles-lettres*, which would have justified your concern about any possible historical embellishment. But more to the point, the event was witnessed by over seventy men and boys—all of whom are God fearing—and all of them, those of who are still living, will tell the tale exactly as I have written it here. They will swear to you, Senors and Senoras (you will notice I did not include the title, Senorita, for I have forbidden unmarried women from reading this)—that, indeed, the spectacle took the better part of two hours. The ten or so witnesses, those men who are no longer living, will have to be questioned in another life.

A month later the whore left town. Everyone assumed it had been her humiliation that drove her from Tizimin. That was partly true—for she was seldom seen outside her room—but it wasn't the whole story. To her dismay, she had learned she was carrying a child. She knew her own cycle well enough to believe none of the men in town could be responsible. During those days, when she was at risk, she worked on her knees. A lot of men liked that best anyway and she didn't have to waste time taking men to her room, for she could work in the cantinas or any place where she could find a little privacy and a soft place to kneel. She believed the old doctor had made a mistake and she had every intention of calling him when her period finally came—she'd tell the old fool a thing or two. The only coupling that had resulted in an ejaculation inside her—during the worst day of her cycle, as it happens—had been with the stallion. This information was recounted to me on the doctor's deathbed, which accounts for this lapse of his oath of confidentiality. He was desperate for my opinion as I had been his attorney for a great many years. I told him that no woman is meticulous about her cycle and most certainly one of us had fathered a bastard. He was greatly relieved after my pronouncement, which perplexed me for he was the medical expert, not I. He died of old age—for which he had no cure—and his death took place not long after the whore left town. You may trust that deathbed confessions have the ring of truth.

Two decades passed. Nothing changed much in Tizimin. People were born and people died. One day a beautiful whore arrived in town. This is an event that would normally go unrecorded.

Eloisa arrived with a battered suitcase and a perfect face. As perfect as the face on one of the Holy Virgins painted by Ignacio Zuloaga. At the risk of being blasphemous, I have to state that I have never understood how God could grant whores such beauty while at the same time tolerating visages that can frighten small children to exist on some of our wives, women who have led nothing but the purist lives. I said perfect—and I stand firm by that—although we soon noticed a small birthmark on her forehead. It was shaped like a small star but no one thought it spoiled her otherwise consummate face. She had quick and responsive eyes, which were almost black, and her hair was blacker than any hair we had ever seen, even blacker than the hair on some of the Guatemalan Maya. She wore it in a ponytail, which is a style that isn't common in Mexico. The ponytail was long, falling well past her waist and when she moved, it switched around in a very sexy manner. The men speculated she was no more than nineteen years old.

The whore had strange habits. We Yucatacos know whores and are seldom surprised by them. After all, the first whore in Mexico—Malinali—was a Yucataca. But none of the men had ever seen a whore exercise before. Whores are lazy by nature, experience told the men that. But Eloisa ran each morning. She would leave her room dressed in running clothes and would run—some said five miles or so. The town dogs, which were usually lazier than the whores and always docile with humans, ran after her, barking frantically, attempting to bite at her ankles, but she ran so fast they couldn't keep up with her. For she had a sound heart and lungs. To look at her was to know she had a perfect conformation for running: long tapered legs, hind quarters well rounded and muscled, and good feet.

And she was a *vegetariana*, which seemed equally strange to the men. Most of them were unsure what that meant, exactly, but one man who reads all the popular magazines suggested such a diet was responsible for her calm temperament. She ate salads and grains, carrots, apples, and the like. She drank only water—even when she was in the cantinas. What kind of whore drinks nothing but water? Her only indulgence seemed to be sugar cubes, which she carried in a pocket and she could be seen occasionally popping one into her mouth.

Eloisa quickly became the most popular whore in town. In fact, she rejected two marriage proposals. Men never expect a whore to have a tight vagina, but hers was cavernous. Normally that would be held against her—a point they might have used to achieve a reduction of her price—but what made an hour with her so desirable, in spite of her cavernous size, was the superb muscle control of her vagina. It could tighten around the smallest *pinga*, like a python playing with a small rodent.

She could always be found in the cantinas or on the streets looking for men to take back to her small room, which was in a boarding house run by a widow who was rumored to have murdered her husband and hidden his body. Otherwise, where was he? The other whores constantly had hangovers, or real or imagined ills that kept them from working every day; but not her. The worst she had was a little colic once in a while.

When she had the adoration of all the men in town, she began boasting. Not harmless boasting, the way many of the girls boasted: My tits are the biggest in Tizimin, or the most shapely, or they have the least sag. No, this was a boast they had heard before, but not for many years. She boasted that she could tire out a stallion. The boasting went on and on and eventually the men tired of hearing it.

One morning four men came to her room; they woke her and forced her to dress, then told her she was to be taken to a hacienda that bred horses. The old Ford truck had been replaced with a newer model, which had air-conditioning, so all four men decided to squeeze into the cab. Since there was no one to watch her they tied her hands to the inside of the tailgate so she couldn't jump out of the rear of the truck if she chose to. If she jumped they would have to go back and search for her. The main road to Yasihon is now paved and the trip takes less than an hour, half the time of the first whore's journey. Still, it was hot.

At the hacienda, she was led to a small corral. Some of the men, who were old enough to have witnessed a similar contest years before, told her what was expected of her. They told her how to plead if the horse became too much for her and, after she pleaded, they would remove the horse from the corral. They expressed their sincere hope that this would cure her boasting once and for all.

Eloisa said she knew of a horse that had gotten the best of another whore many years before. Was that horse still living? She was told that it had been retired to a back pasture as it was too mean to be around humans. She asked to see it. Why not, they said, but you will be up against a much younger horse. They led her to the pasture and she jumped over the fence as the horse approached. They screamed for her to get out, as the horse was believed to be a killer. When the horse came close, she reached out her hand and the horse nuzzled it. She put her arms around its head and whispered to it. She gave it some of her sugar cubes. This went on for a long time but the men tired of the display; after all, they were excited and wanted to see her inside the corral.

Back at the corral, she was told to remove her clothes before climbing up onto the wooden platform. I wasn't a bit surprised to see the original platform, for things are not casually discarded in Mexico, although it had likely been put to other uses, such as serving as a storage platform for drying beans or aging cheeses. She slowly turned around so the men could inspect her—most of them had only seen her without clothes in her dimly lit room and had only guessed at how exceptional she was. Her breasts and nipples rivaled the sweetmeats and caramels in The Paseo de Montejo confectioneries' windows. Her pubic hair was so black and lustrous that a man who had never pressed against its softness might suspect it was carved out of obsidian.

She got down in the straw and a blanket from a broodmare was placed over her back.

A breeding hobble was placed around her neck, then threaded under her belly, back to her legs, and adjusted to her size. Hock straps were attached to the back of her knees, then secured to the hobble. The men, believing they were finished, started to move away but she stopped them by asking them to please use a Scotch hobble, preferably on her left leg. They mistakenly believed she only wanted her legs parted so as to be able to flaunt her glorious vagina to them, for they couldn't fathom any other reason for the request. I believe I was the only one who guessed her true motive. But I shouldn't feel so smug for most of the time I, like other men, am usually mistaken about the motives of women; our wives are mysterious enough, how can we hope to understand whores, the most enigmatic of all women?

By now a hundred men from Tizimin had arrived and the wagering began. Many of the men had lost wages the first time, or remembered that their fathers or uncles had bet on the other whore—after all, we Yucatacos are many things, but first and foremost we are true romantics, until we learn otherwise. So the patron of the hacienda had to offer odds of ten to one before the men would agree to bet. Then the whore called out, I have ten thousand pesos in the pocket of my jeans. Since I cannot move, would one of you please get it—and bet it for me? At first no one moved but then a boy of about twelve squeezed between the rails and got into the corral, to the place where the jeans were lying in the dust, along with her T-shirt and panties. He found the pesos crumpled together in a pocket. She smiled at him and the boy fell hopelessly in love with her. He wanted to steal her panties but he couldn't imagine himself the possessor of such a treasure. Where would he keep them? In a pirate's chest along with diamonds, gold, and silver? The woman he would eventually marry would never know the source of his melancholy.

Two men brought an appaloosa stallion to the corral, for it took two men to control the beast. The smell from the blanket had it kicking and bucking, desperate to get into the corral. They led it inside but it broke away from them and quickly mounted the whore. Its huge member slid into her in one quick, long stroke.

The appaloosa attempted to place its teeth on the whore's neck to hold her in position—a horse in a large corral will do that to a mare—not understanding that the hobble made it impossible for her to resist. When the horse found it could move in and out of her at will, and she was making no attempt to flee, it lost interest in her neck. The horse settled into a rhythm of long, violent strokes, which the whore absorbed as if the beast were just one more paying customer. The men were transfixed at the sight. Even those of us who had witnessed the first contest were as spellbound as we had been the first time.

An hour passed. The patron wasn't worried for he remembered that the first whore had also lasted an hour. He knew that it was the second hour that had gotten to her.

Eloisa had watched the sun move across the sky and calculated that an hour had passed. She was awash in semen from the horse but no doubt she welcomed it because the semen helped lubricate her. Did she sense the horse was slowing down, that it wasn't penetrating her as deeply as it had during the first hour? Still, she must also have been tiring and she knew she had a long way to go if she were to win her bet for herself against the horse.

The second hour passed and her lover—I feel strongly that she had begun to think of the horse as her lover—hadn't hinted at the possibility of giving up.

Then, suddenly, the stallion began withdrawing, its proud member as limp as a maricon's wrist. The patron, who stood to lose heavily if the beast didn't continue, came into the corral and took a crop to it—but it couldn't be persuaded to go on. The horse was now as tame as a kitten.

The patron spat and said, *Cagejon*! But he began paying off the men who had bet on the whore. She had dressed and, although she was wobbly on her legs, she joined the line. When he got to her, he was unhappy but gracious. Come, I have more money inside the house, he said. You had a large bet.

The main house at the hacienda is heavily shuttered on the inside to keep it dark and cool. I have been invited to this house a number of times and I can state that, although it has many good qualities, it lacks a woman's touch. The patron has never married. Elaborately framed portraits of his ancestors hang on the walls. I asked him once if he regretted not having a son who might commission an artist to come and paint the patron's portrait? Since that is the way it is done in that family. When the patron saw the whore looking at the dark portraits he said, I suppose it's comforting to know who your ancestors were. Most caballeros don't know their fathers' names. She wanted to say, I know who my father is, but she knew the patron wasn't being snobbish—although he had had a university education—he was simply being factual.

An Indian servant girl appeared and, just as he was about to dismiss her, he thought to ask the whore, Do you need any salve? You must need some? The girl can find some for you. It wasn't that he felt guilty at what had happened—far from it. If he thought he could get away with it, he would have marched her back to the corral, sore or not, and selected a worthier horse, a horse that would win his money back. But she was in his house and he respected the timeless Mexican tradition of treating everyone who is invited into a man's house as an honored guest. He was relieved when she refused his offer—he really had no desire to watch a whore palliate herself.

When he took a moneybox from the drawer of an old desk, she

asked, How much is the old black stallion? He was surprised at the question but he said, Do you have a ranch? She said, Yes, a small ranch in the north of Mexico. Near Saucillo. He tried to place Saucillo but couldn't. We don't race our horses that far north, he replied finally. Then the patron said the black stallion was ten thousand pesos, although they both knew he would probably have given it away. Then she asked him to set a price on the appaloosa. Ninety thousand pesos, he replied. It would be worth more but it has been disgraced. No disrespect, Senorita. Anyone who knew horses would know it was worth closer to eighty—even before it had been disgraced—but she didn't want to bargain with him. The total for the two horses was exactly the amount of her winnings—she would have been surprised if he had made it less.

I want both horses, she said.

They're a handful, he replied, do you have caballeros at the ranch to help you with them?

No, she answered, there is only me and my mother. But we will manage.

No one has ventured from Tizimin to Saucillo to see if the horses arrived safely and if the two women are, as the whore said—managing. The women may have found that horses are more like men than they had hoped, with the same failings: foul moods, inattentiveness, perplexity, and general cussedness. I confess that I am too old to make such a long trip but we have many young men in town who travel to Merida, and beyond, as if it were an ordinary thing to do.

No, what discourages us from making the trip is not the great distance, although that is a consideration, but rather it's the likelihood that Eloisa gave a false address so that none of us could, if we ever chose to, drop by to pay our respects.

SHRINE OF GUADALUPE, LOURDES, VICTORIA'S SECRET

❧

The alarm went off at 5:00 AM. When Pedro woke up he sensed the ghost in the room. "Why don't you turn off the alarm for me?" he shouted at it. The alarm continued ringing. One thing about ghosts— they never do anybody a favor.

He got up and turned off the alarm. The clock was on the other side of the room from the bed so he wasn't tempted to reach over and perhaps fall back to sleep. He made a cup of coffee for himself—the only nourishment he had in the mornings since Rosaria's death. He dressed, went out the door with his mug of coffee, and walked to the beach.

He was an old man—nearly eighty—and he knew if he didn't reach the goal he had set for himself soon, it would be too late. But today was St. Febrona's Feast Day. A good day to find the 100th pair?

The beach along San Miguel was a mile away. He had to be there just as dawn broke, or his competition would beat him to the best objects. The younger men used metal detectors, which they swept back and forth as they walked the beach. Pedro had nothing but contempt for machines like that. Although his vision was failing, he still had the best eyes on the beach. Even the men with the metal detectors admitted to that.

A man could make a living just by collecting and reselling the things the tourists lost or discarded. With seemingly little concern for money they bought things they couldn't possibly take back home with them on an airplane and, when it was time to depart, they simply left their acquisitions on the beach or in the hotel rooms.

One of the most common items left behind was a small surfboard tourists bought for their children. Pedro cleaned the boards and sold them to a store that resold them as new merchandise—for most of them had been used only a few times and some of them had never been in the water. He also found T-shirts, shoes, money, jewelry, sunglasses, and every once in a while a wallet, but mostly he found all the paraphernalia tourists, before leaving, had convinced themselves they couldn't do without.

It is believed that the Mayan language never developed locutions such as how is the weather today? This happens—or, more accurately, doesn't happen—in cultures where the weather is virtually perfect every day. Similarly, Pedro and the other Cozumal natives are blind to the beauty of their surroundings. They have no other frame of reference, and blue skies seem as commonplace to them as does the smog to the residents of Mexico City. As the tourist planes, heading home, bank to the north and pass momentarily over the endless blue water— the water's reflection shimmers on the windows of the plane—the passengers feel the loss of this paradise as if it were a physical pain in their chests. Pedro can't imagine their pain. No, his kinship is with the Maya who beachcombed the same sands centuries before him. His ancestors found crabs, mussels, and clams whereas he finds T-shirts and boogie boards.

He also finds women's panties.

He brought home the first pair six years ago—when Rosaria was still living—and his wife had refused to launder them. He had seen panties in the sand before and had left them where they lay, but this pair was a particularly lovely shade of violet and he had been unwilling to leave them.

"Only a whore would leave her panties on the beach," Rosaria had said.

Pedro doubted the woman was a whore—at least in the sense Rosaria meant—but simply a woman who couldn't find her panties in the dark, a woman who had chosen a lover who wasn't patient enough to help her. (Pedro concluded later that, if there had been no moon or stars the night before, his chances of finding a pair of panties increased.)

He had laundered them himself and at first he kept them in a tackle box he no longer used since he had stopped fishing. Inside the panties he noticed a label—Victoria's Secret—which he was unable to read or translate since he knew no English.

A few weeks later he found a second pair with the same Victoria's Secret label. He knew Rosaria wouldn't launder them but it didn't matter, he would do it himself. "What do you want them for?" Rosaria had said when she saw him at the sink. "Don't you know a whore left them behind?"

For the last year of her life Rosaria had been confined to her bed. Rheumatism had crippled her and Pedro had cared for her during that year. Considering all the gentle care he had given her, he couldn't understand why her ghost haunted him. She had been dead four years now.

He was disappointed if a week went by when he didn't find any panties. With each pair he tried to imagine what had happened on that spot of sand the night before. He was certain that the gringa tourists had lain with a Mexican as he couldn't imagine beautiful gringas slipping their panties off for their husbands, not for those pale skinned creatures who talked on their cell phones all day.

He now had 99 pair. Occasionally he found panties with other labels but he left them behind for they didn't fit into his very select collection. Besides, the other panties were always less beautiful, and so must have been the women who lost them.

After Rosaria died, he took pins from her sewing basket and began pinning the panties flat on the walls of the one room house. Pink, white, blue, yellow, black, red and violet panties added as much color to the room as would a dozen vases of flowers. There was no house in the neighborhood that was so gaily decorated. Children came to see the decoration and they were in awe at the profusion of color. Older women, however, felt the need to form the sign of the cross as they passed by the front of the house.

The only dispute he and Rosaria had ever had in all their married years was over the likely profession of the women whose panties he brought home. Were they whores—as she believed—or just moonstruck women—as he believed? As soon as he found the 100th pair he thought he knew how he would resolve that dispute. Of course Rosaria wouldn't be there to acknowledge her triumph or defeat when he gave her the news—but perhaps her ghost could find peace at last.

Rosaria's rheumatism had developed when she was a young woman and it had dampened her enthusiasm for sex. If Pedro had had the money he would have spent it on whores. Having no money, he relied on dreams in which he would present himself at the front door of a brothel and they would know his name and remember him from his frequent visits to the establishment.

"Senor Pedro, so nice to see you again. The girls ask for you every day."

The girls at the brothel would wear only Victoria's Secret panties.

One morning as he was retrieving a pair of panties from the sand a young man with a metal detector informed him that the Victoria's Secret store was in Brownsville, Texas. The man had seen it on a visit to the States. (Neither of them understood that it was a chain of stores.) Pedro promised himself he would visit the store.

Over the years he had developed a serious limp. In order to minimize the pain he felt in his left hip he would drag his leg rather than lift it. He had no money to spend on doctors. Any extra money would have been spent on whores, not doctors. His priest assured him his limp would almost certainly be cured if he made a pilgrimage to the Shrine of the Virgin of Guadalupe at Tepeyac. His priest had also told him about Lourdes in France. Pedro listened to the priest's stories of the miracles that happen at holy sites. Although he didn't say anything, Pedro knew people—crippled and ill—who had visited Tepayac and they were no better off when they returned home than they were when they left. During those years he became convinced that the limp—which was becoming even more pronounced—could be cured by a visit to Victoria's Secret.

As he approached his 80th year he realized the futility of trying to repair a body as old as his. He would still go to Brownsville, but no longer looking for a cure. A new plan formed in his mind. He would present all the panties he had collected to the owner of the store. Although he had laundered them carefully he doubted the owner would buy them to resell as new panties. But, if the owner did want them for resale, he hoped he could enter into an arrangement whereby he could make a yearly trip to deliver them.

No matter what happened, he would get to see the women who shopped at the store and by doing so resolve the dispute with Rosaria. Yes, the trip would determine who the women were, the ones who left their panties on the beach and went back to their rooms with sand on their asses. Didn't their husbands wonder where all the sand in their beds came from?

He had saved enough money for a bus ticket to Matamoros, the town just across the border from Brownsville. He knew he would have to walk across the border but surely the guards, once they understood the importance of his trip, would let him cross? The man at the Puerto Morelos bus station had told him it would take at least a week to get to

Matamoros after changing buses in a dozen places. He said it would be a long hot trip that might kill an eighty-year-old man.

Pedro didn't want to die on a bus. But he would be content to die at the Victoria's Secret store, if God willed it. A man can't plan his own death—that responsibility God reserves for himself. Yet if a man were able to plan it, what better than to lie down on the soft carpet in the Victoria's Secret lingerie department where beautiful women are replacing the panties they have lost on the beaches of the world—and there take his last breaths?

CARLOTA TRIES HER BEST

I've never worn glasses and I can state for the record that for a man my age, I can see just fine—excessive masturbation as a young man notwithstanding. Why do I bring this up? Because my eyesight had been questioned. I left her room just before midnight last New Year's Eve and was walking down the hallway, rather mindlessly whistling a tune I remembered from my university days—although the title now escapes me—and I was about to pass the room where Roberto had spent the last hour, when the door opened.

I'm not one to snoop, far from it, but the hallway was somewhat dark and the light from within drew my eyes. Roberto was just leaving and, as he turned to give Brigitte a farewell kiss, I managed to get a fleeting glimpse of her. *My God*, I thought, *she's a woman in her late 60s? More gray than blond.* Knowing his taste in women—and the high reputation of the brothel—I was taken aback.

When I cautiously mentioned this to him later he said, "You are quite mistaken. She was very much the Brigitte Bardot of the year Bardot made *And God Created Woman.* Barely twenty-two." By his own account he had viewed the film 1,000 times; one assumes he knew what she looked like. Then he said, "It would be impossible that I should be the one who is mistaken, my old friend, since Brigitte and I spent a most wonderful hour together—I suggest you schedule an examination with your optometrist." (I had spent an hour with Sharon Stone.)

Long time intimates of this brothel will know that once a year, on New Year's Eve, the establishment closes its door to all but a select few. No reservations are taken. If a man believes he needs a reservation then surely he knows he isn't welcome. It's like the old joke about Commadore Vanderbilt's yacht. If you have to ask what it costs, you can't afford it.

Yes, New Year's Eve at the brothel is expensive: 25,000 pesos. But that price hasn't varied in the twenty years I have spent my New Year's Eves there. I know the patron's costs must have risen in that time but he is too much the gentleman to pass his increases on to his loyal habitues. That is the practice department stores employ. Yet these actresses certainly don't work for minimal wages—no, they are too accomplished in their craft for that.

On this one night, the patron dismisses his whores—who are girls of mostly mediocre talent—and replaces them with what I assume are actresses of exceptional ability. I say actresses for I don't know what else to call them. They are whores, yes, but the fact that they are capable of impersonating another person so completely—if that is what it is they do—makes me believe that they must have had extensive training in the theatre.

There is only one rule we all must adhere to. We are allowed an hour with the woman of our dreams, but not one more minute than that. We must be out of her room before the stroke of midnight or, as the patron says, "I will not take responsibility for the consequences." That is certainly ominous but we respect the rule—not because we fear the unknown, but because rules are meant to be followed.

Once, when the patron had had too much to drink, he admitted to me that the genesis for the New Year's Evenings had not originated with him, but with a gypsy who worked for him—a man called Santos. At first the patron had been reluctant to add this feature but, fortunately for us, the gypsy had convinced him the evenings would distinguish the brothel. It had once been the custom for all brothels to employ gypsies, for they possess qualities that make them ideal employees. They are discreet, inventive, and impervious to the whores' incessant complaints. They're also capable of using quick and decisive force when that is required, as it is from time to time, when men of the wrong sort visit the brothels. Of course, whores—who are superstitious and self-deceiving by nature—believe gypsies made a pact with *el diablo* himself. To hear the whores tell it, they made that pact centuries ago.

Last year, when I was with Senorita Stone, I made the mistake of calling her Catherine, the name she used in *Basic Instinct*. I had asked that she be dressed and—how should I say this? also undressed—as she was in that famous movie. She sat on a straight back chair with her legs crossed—but pliant—as if she were back at that police station. Then she corrected me and said, "Please, call me Sharon." Childishly I was going to pretend to be Detective Nick Curran for an hour, but that became unnecessary for I was soon convinced that my tired out, sixty-five-year-old body was the only one she wanted to interrogate her.

Then it dawned on me. Yes, the patron certainly hires actresses for that evening, but he is clever enough to know that we will almost certainly pick a blond one. This makes his task easier. Furthermore, we undoubtedly let it slip during one of our visits just who it was we would be likely to choose the following New Year's Eve . . .

So, for the past year, I have said nothing about whom my choice will be.

When Roberto and I arrive at the brothel it is approximately 10:00 PM. The patron greets us warmly. We have just come from having dinner at Estoril where I enjoyed the sea bass in fresh coriander sauce. The patron always dresses for New Year's Eve in a suit that must be forty years old, yet it is immaculate and the tailoring cannot be easily duplicated these days. He makes the rest of us appear that we buy our suits off the rack.

We share a glass of champagne with the patron, for it is still forty-five minutes before 11:00. We talk mostly of politics. The patron immigrated from Spain nearly fifty years ago and he still follows the parliamentary elections there. We sit in comfortable club chairs in a room that was decorated at the turn of the last century in the rather cluttered, heavy taste of the time. Some of the younger men have commented that the place should be remodeled, but fortunately the patron ignores that kind of talk.

The brothel is located in the southern part of the capitol, in a section of the Coyoacan district, a neighborhood that is no longer fashionable. But it was fashionable in my father's time and it had been one of the better addresses in my grandfather's. A few months ago I took my grandson to visit Diego Rivera's house and studio. As we drove along Insurgentes, we chanced to pass by the street on which the brothel sits— an omen perhaps? My grandson is old enough to be introduced to the patron. He is actually older than I was when I was taken there by my father. My son doesn't like the brothel, he prefers to use the services of the escort agencies that advertise in the local newspapers. Participation in the New Year's Eve parties would skip a generation—if I'm successful with my grandson—but that will allow him to marry safely; a boring woman if he chooses. He will still be able to enjoy the women of his dreams, even if it is only once a year.

When it's finally time to announce our choices for the evening, my friend asks for a girl whose name I barely recognize but whom I believe is a young American pop star. Blond, of course. You are making it too easy for him, I think, but say nothing. Actually, my friend is my senior by a few years and the idea of him with a sixteen-year-old girl is stimulating. When it's my turn, I say to the patron, "I'd like to spend an hour with the Empress Carlota."

"Excellent!" he exclaims. I can tell by his expression that he truly approves of my selection. Just then the gypsy comes over to us and the patron asks him which room the empress occupies. "Room fourteen," he replies.

As I climb the stairs to her room, I doubt the patron will be able to pull this one off. My choice had to be unexpected and, of course, Carlota wasn't blond. There was more than that, obviously, for she has been dead for over 70 years.

I knock on her door with a timidity I haven't felt since I was a virgin. She answers my knock, in French—"*Vous avez la permission d'entre*"—and I realize, yes, of course, it must be she; French was her first language! If I remember correctly, she had not mastered much Spanish, let alone the nuances used here in Mexico.

"*Merci. Je m'appel* Carlos, *mon imperatice*," I say, as I am quite comfortable in her native tongue.

I open the door. My, God, she's breathtaking! I knew her, of course, from the painting of her by the Belgian artist, Portaels, which hangs at Miramar. She is wearing the very dress she had worn for the artist. But she is even lovelier in person, if that is possible, for artists are known for flattery. The dress is the Lombardic national costume, heavily brocaded, with a narrow bodice that is cut cleverly to show her delicious bosom. The skirt is full, over crinolines that she lifts slightly as she walks. She had been described as an "Italian type beauty" with "magnolia skin and dark luminous eyes." She is all of that.

She comes right to the point. "I know what this place is and why I am here. I'm quite willing to be your lover for an hour but only if you promise you will do everything in your power to help the emperor."

"Yes, of course, empress."

"Thank God," she says, clearly relieved.

"Whatever I can do."

"Do you have any influence with Juarez?"

"That remains to be seen."

"Imagine that little Indian raising an army!"

"A rag tag bunch."

"I don't know why the people of Mexico have turned on us."

"Nor, I, your majesty."

"Yet I knew from the cold reception we received in Veracruz we had been misled."

"Veracruz has never been known for its hospitality."

"No, it was more than that. The conservatives and Napoleon III—they were all deluded."

"Mexico wants a republic."

"It's godless radicalism."

"The republicans have acted brutally, I must admit."

"Is it true that they intend to execute Max?"

"They captured the emperor at Queretaro, empress."

"But you do support us? You're a monarchist?"

"I became one the day I saw your portrait."

"The one at Miramar?"

"Yes."

"You've been there, then?"

"Once, when I was a student."

"The artist was in love with me."

"How could he not be?"

"He begged me to allow him to kiss the hem of my dress. And lick the toes of my shoes."

"And did you let him?"

"The more important question is, would that satisfy you?"

"I hate to disappoint your majesty, but I want, shall I say—all of you."

She looks me directly in the eyes. "Very well, that should demonstrate the sincerity of my appeal to you."

"I will take it as such."

"I have an audience with the pope whom I expect will intervene on our behalf."

"Which pope?" I couldn't remember who had been pope in 1867.

"Why, Pius XIV, of course. Aren't you Catholic? I don't know if I could make love to a man who isn't Catholic."

"I assure you I am."

"And you will help? Even if the pope refuses?"

"I will do everything I can for the emperor."

"Then let me demonstrate our—my—gratitude."

She gets down on her knees in front of me in a most unempresslike fashion, her skirts spread out like a stupendous flower. She looks up at me, then removes her fan shaped tiara and tosses it aside. Her dark hair is parted in the middle and pulled tight over her ears. I start to say, Empress, are you sure you want . . . but before I can speak she has found my fly and quickly has me in her mouth. Then she begins uttering terms of endearment—mostly in 19th century French slang although "*ma petite sucrerie*" is still in usage. Those are words I am frankly surprised the empress knows, let alone that she will repeat with her mouth full.

I am fearful that I will spill my seed too soon. At my age, it isn't usually possible to have a repeat performance in the same evening and I want to climb between her legs more than I have ever wanted anything in my life. I begin to pull myself out of her regal mouth. She resists me—instinctually knowing the reason for my attempted withdrawal—saying, "I assure you, once I shed this dress you will have no problem bedding me."

With her encouragement, I let myself go. The empress doesn't spill a drop, which is a testament to the etiquette of her peerless breeding. In my joy, I utter the basest French slang. I suddenly think of Roberto—who learned his English at Cambridge—for he must have been conversing with Britany, or whatever her name was, and they must be doing so in hideous American teenage slang. Roberto is exceptionally well endowed and when she saw it for the first time and considered its measure, I wondered if she thought it was "cool" or "far out" or something like that.

Carlota and I quickly undress. Her silk undergarments—although old fashioned in design—are not so different from the ones my mother wore. I used to treasure the moments when I saw them, and I always found it possible to be near my mother's room at the hour when she dressed. (When I reached the age of twelve she felt it was prudent to close her doors to me.) Carlota stands naked under the soft light from the chandelier, her skin ghostly pale. It isn't the pale skin one associates with whores; it has none of the corrosion that comes from having had too many hands touch it. I think: this woman has lived in equatorial Mexico but her skin has never seen the sun.

Our clothes are as entwined on the floor as I hope our bodies will soon be. We jump, gloriously naked, onto the antique four poster and it creaks but holds. As an economy, the brothel no longer uses Porthault sheets during the year, but the patron makes sure each bed is made up with them on New Year's Eve.

I say something about its being New Year's Eve and she replies, "Are you mad? It's June." Of course it would be June in her mind. That was the month in which Maximillian was executed.

She spreads her legs and I crawl between them. Her royal bush—I'm interested to see—is as wet as a commoner's. There is no hint of my impotence and her hips are bucking in anticipation. I am shaking—much as Max must have been when he asked King Leopold for her hand. One guesses Max was also shaking when he first climbed between those very same pale thighs.

"I do love Max," she says as I kiss her.

"And I love you, your majesty," I reply.

The scent of her body is admittedly strong—in her century even women of her class seldom bathed, preferring to use French perfumes to disguise their odors. Modern women, in their desire for what is an artificial cleanliness, have lost this true sense of womanhood. But not my darling Carlota. Her scent is an aphrodisiac.

We couple vigorously for the better part of an hour. Fortunately the rooms are soundproofed for her screams of ecstasy, her vile denouncements of Napoleon III, and the noises the bed makes would have brought everyone into the room to see if either a riot or a massacre was occurring. We rock the bed back and forth—indeed, it moves four or five feet away from the wall until it comes to rest against a large chest of drawers.

We lay back, spent. Her pale skin is flush with color; it's as if I have pumped life into her along with my seed. Her head rests on my shoulder.

I say, "Empress?"

"Yes?" she replies sleepily.

"I have a house on the gulf—near a town called Progreso."

"And where is that?"

"In the Yucatan."

"But only Indians live there?"

"That is no longer true."

"Still."

"The house is quite modern, I assure you."

"So?"

"Come with me? I want to live there with you."

"And leave Max? I couldn't."

"I know the patron. I've never asked for a favor before—"

"And why would you ask him?"

"But you must work—have an arrangement with him? Do you not? I would have to ask."

"I work for no one. Or, perhaps I should say I work on behalf of my subjects—the people of Mexico."

"But Max is doomed. You will no longer be empress."

"Never say that! There is always the pope!"

"Juarez won't listen to the pope."

"A direct appeal? Surely?"

"But I love you as much as Max does!"

"To be honest, I'm not sure he loves me. But I love him."

"You have just found a man who loves you."

"You only want me because with me you are able to perform twice in an hour."

"I admit, you do make me feel like a young man again, Carlota."

"I never gave you permission to use my name!"

"No, no, of course not. You're my empress. I'll never forget that."

"See that you don't. Or I shall have to ask you to leave."

"If I leave without you, you may never escape this whoredom."

"Do you think what we did tonight makes me a whore?"

"It's not what I believe, rather it's what the patron believes that matters." *Or, more likely*, I think, *the gypsy*. I'm beginning to understand.

"I fear only Juarez."

"You'll end up servicing an endless line of men."

"It will be worth it if one of them helps Max."

"Gather up your clothes! We'll leave here together!"

"I can't."

"It's almost 1999. A new year. A new beginning, your majesty!"

"There you go again! I tell you it's June! The year of our Lord, 1867."

"At my house, I've adopted the Yucatecan habit of sleeping in a hammock. They sleep two, you know? There is always a cool breeze off the water."

"You would have to be in love to sleep in a hammock—since you would be pressed so tightly together."

"I can't wait for us to share one!"

"It will never happen."

A chorus of fireworks goes off. "Empress, that fireworks is to celebrate the New Year. You must believe me!"

"It's gunfire," she says, getting up from the bed. She throws back the heavy curtains.

I join her. I can see a half-dozen boys in the street lighting fire-crackers. A car passes and one of the boys throws a firecracker at it. "See?" I say.

"See what?" she replies. "Those men with their rifles belong to Juarez. I have no doubt of that."

"What?"

"Standing over there by their horses. How filthy the street is. Remind me to have it paved when this is over."

The street is, of course, paved. The boys move under a street light and their modern clothes are evident. "See how they are dressed?" I say.

"Yes," she replies. "Max would never allow our soldiers to wear those pajama-like pants."

"Calzones?"

"Yes, I believe that's what they're called."

"But those boys are wearing blue jeans," I protest.

"Do you question me?"

"Empress, do you realize we are having our first lover's quarrel?"

"Max and I never quarrel." She closes the curtains. "Now, you've been sweet, but I must get some rest. I'm to see the pope tomorrow."

I look at my watch. Ten minutes to midnight. I can still hear the sound of fireworks coming in through the window. We return to the sweat soaked bed and lie side by side. "We made a mess of this bed," she says. "We have somehow torn one of the sheets."

"The maid will come in the morning," I whisper to her. I wonder: is she merely a convincing actress or have I unwittingly brought Carlota back for my pleasure, only to leave her stranded here? But that is mad-ness! And what is even more insane, if the Brigitte Bardot I saw was truly a sixty-year-old woman, then to others is Carlota—dead over sev-enty years—nothing but bones? Fifty thousand Mexicans died liber-ating our land from her husband and I care nothing about them—I care only for her. I realize she is willing to whore with a thousand men if she believes they will aid her cause, and I can do nothing about it. I look at my watch again. Five minutes to midnight. I can tell from the sound of her breathing that she is sleeping. I want to kiss the part of her that will wear out before she rescues her husband, but she has turned over on her stomach. I am able to kiss her on the forehead before I get up from the bed, dress and leave, closing the door as quietly as possible so as not to wake her.

Roberto is just leaving his room as I pass by. He calls my name softly—as if the whores might open their doors if he were to speak out loud—and I stop. "I did something I thought I'd never do," he whispers. There are other men leaving other rooms, nodding politely as they pass us. The gypsy is standing at the far end of the hallway, smoking a cigarette.

"And what is that?" I say in a normal tone.

"I asked Britany to come and live with me. At my house in Cuernavaca. Carlos, you can't imagine how it was with her."

"And she agreed?"

"Unfortunately, no."

"Does she have someone else?" My thoughts turn to Carlota and Max.

"No, apparently not."

"What, then?"

"You won't believe it—but she has a record deal."

"And what is that?"

"A contract to make a musical recording."

"And that is more important than being with a man who loves her?"

"It's 1999, Carlos. I'm afraid we no longer understand the world." He thinks about what he has just said. "No, perhaps it's just whores that we don't understand?"

WHO, ME?

It can be said, without fear of contradiction, that Guglielmita loves men. Ah, but there is a catch. For although Guglielmita loves men, it seems her dearest bodily part is of the opposite opinion. All too frequently— and just at the height of passion—a man might be forced to hurriedly extricate himself, crying out, your *chocho* just bit me! Or, before a man even got started, he might blurt out, senorita, your *chocho* just hissed at me. Unfortunately, like women who are incapable of believing that their children are out of control in the supermarket or at the theatre, she paid little attention to these complaints.

When her *chocho* acted out in some particularly displeasing, spiteful, or even harmful way and her customer complained, Guglielmita would sit up and peer down between her legs, a questioning look on her pretty face. Of course, her *chocho* would by then be on its best behavior, smiling innocently (no wonder *chochos* have earned the nickname, mother of all saints). If it had been capable of speaking it would have said, Who, me? Lying back down, Guglielmita would say, You're imagining things. Put your pinga back in. Her customer would be tempted, for her bed was a soft hammock and her arms were waiting to hold him tightly to her—but he had the safety of his manhood to consider. At that point, he would more likely be inclined just to toss a few pesos on the floor and leave.

Of all the men Guglielmita loved—and there were many—there was only one she hoped would one day pop the question. His name was Arnaldo

Arnaldo could see himself married to Guglielmita but he, too, was put off by her *chocho's* decidedly antisocial behavior. One day, looking at himself in the mirror while he was shaving, he decided he wasn't getting any younger. His moustache, which was his best feature, so everyone said, was turning gray. He was tired of living alone—well, he did have his dogs—so he decided to do something he, or some other man, should have done years before.

Arnaldo correctly deduced that her *chocho* was in serious need of training. As it happens, Arnaldo was a dog trainer by profession—which is why he had this insight. And therefore, of all the men who visited Guglielmita, he was probably the only one who not only knew what was required to solve this gynecic behavioral problem, but was also the only one who stood a chance of success. As every man knows, there are many women who don't train their *chochos*, allowing them to exist in a state of what Arnaldo, as a dog trainer, called perpetual maladaptive playfulness.

Arnaldo continued looking into the mirror. Now he saw a sadness in his eyes he hadn't noticed before. Yes, Guglielmita would be a comfort to him in his old age. But not if he couldn't do something about her *chocho*.

He hoped she would give up her trade for him. This wouldn't be easy for her. She was the most beautiful woman for miles around and she knew it. Being the most beautiful woman was a considerable feat when you stopped to consider history. Hadn't the propitious mingling of Spanish conquistador and Aztec and Maya genes created—although, yes, it took a couple of centuries—the most beautiful women in all of Christendom? Compared to the women Arnaldo had seen on television or in the movies, Guglielmita had eyes that were blacker, her mouth was more wanton, her hair more wildly extravagant. And those other women were so thin as to be starving. No one looking at Guglielmita's gelatinous ass, breasts, and thighs would believe she was starving. All that bleached blond hair on television! Did the presenters think anyone would truly believe they were *gueras*? Guglielmita's hair was as black as Cortes' heart. And what's more, the women on television dressed like whores while Guglielmita dressed like a lady. Arnaldo had personally driven her many times to the Wal-Mart in Merida to buy clothes. These exceptional qualities accounted for Giglielmita's continued popularity, despite the frequent coitus interruptus her customers experienced. If she were to retire, a hundred men would plead with her to reconsider. He hoped she wouldn't listen. He wanted her to belong to him alone.

Arnaldo wiped the last traces of shaving cream from his face—but he continued to stare into the mirror. Yes, he would take up the challenge. Yet he wouldn't enter into this lightly, oh no, for he, more than most men, knew there was a reason for the adage, you can't teach an old dog new tricks.

Praise would be the key to success. Good *chocho*. Good *chocho*. But he could just hear Guglielmita responding with, What's that you're saying? If he spoke loud enough for her *chocho* to hear, then Guglielmita would surely hear as well? How would she respond?

If he married Guglielmita he would have to give up seeing Zitella. He didn't love Zitella. Still, it would be difficult to give her up. What's more, Zitella's *chocho* was perfectly behaved. One of the ironies of life. Who decides who we love? God, probably. But then, wasn't it also God who gave him a mustache so glorious that Guglielmita preferred him to all the others?

There was so much to consider.

THE ENLIGHTENED PENAL
CODE

Drug offenses are taken very seriously in Guatemala. It shouldn't come as a surprise that after her trial—a trial that lasted no more than twenty minutes—the girl was sentenced to ten years at hard labor. Hard labor here means working in the sugar cane fields eight hours a day, seven days a week. (Please note that convicts are never asked to work on Christmas Day or on September 15, Independence Day.)

Yes, substance abusers can be assured of a swift trial with, shall we say, a predictable outcome? This is never truer than when the accused is a girl with splendid tits and eyes the color of lapis. Our newest convict—Mary Ellen as I shall refer to her—possessed those assets, and more. She was a tall, blond *norteamericana* with hair the color of honey that can only be obtained from manzanita flowers. Splendid tits, eyes like lapis, golden hair—perhaps that description presupposes more than it should, for she wasn't beautiful the way blondes are in, say, Hollywood movies. She had a plain, unpretentious face and she still had the ungainliness that comes with being a teenager. The soft blond fuzz on her tanned arms and legs was characteristic of a younger girl. She wore a T-shirt advertising a rock band, and cut-off jeans, which added to her girlishness.

Don't misunderstand me—she was exceptionally desirable. Certainly the police—who had been following her—thought so. They admired the way her T-shirt moved, as if her splendid tits were made of guayule rubber. It amused them to watch her tug at her tight jeans when they rode up too high, delineating—or so they imagined through their cloudy binoculars—her blond mons veneris. Yes, blondes obsesses us. Particularly in our dreams. How is it that we Guatemalan men, the most romantic and idealistic of lovers, can possess these women only in our sleep? Or, on rare occasions, in our brothels? Is it that the sin of idolatry is so heinous that God decided blondes on this continent should only dwell north of the Rio Grande, among Protestants whose souls are already in jeopardy?

She was with a *norteamericano* boy. Both were carrying backpacks. They had entered Guatemala from Mexico where—we later learned—they had been traveling for over a month. It must have been easy for them to score marijuana along the way, for selling marijuana to American tourists is a way too many Mexicans earn a living. There are also those who make a little money being police informants. This is worth mentioning, for it determined the couple's fate. Sometimes a drug dealer will do both—sell and inform—for this isn't seen as being contradictory, or perverse, but merely as being—to use the popular North American word—entrepreneurial. But Mary Ellen and her boyfriend were ignorant of this. But then, what are Texas college students not ignorant of? Perhaps football, fraternity parties, and hastily performed missionary position sex?

It had been their intention to end up somewhere near the Panama Canal before the summer was over and from there they would fly back to Texas where they would start their second year at one of the universities. Crossing through the Isthmus of Tehuantepec in Mexico, the couple had visited the Maya ruins at Palenque and had lingered there perhaps longer than they had planned, for their supply of marijuana ran out. They located a man who agreed to sell them enough to last a few weeks and they promised to meet him the next morning at the bus station in San Cristobal de las Casas. But that night they met another man—one who had a truck—and for a small fee he agreed to give them a ride to the Mexico/Guatemala border. They were long gone before morning. The first man was so angry when they didn't show up that he turned to his other source of income, he turned them in to the police. Of course, as soon as it was learned that the couple was no longer in Mexico, the man informed our federal police, as he was still hoping for a small reward.

Policemen decided to keep a close eye on them. In very short order, they attempted to purchase marijuana—this was in the main square in

Huehucetenango where that sort of crime is all too prevalent—and we descended upon them. In the confusion surrounding the bust, Mary Ellen's boyfriend got away (it is believed he later managed to slip into Belize). Mary Ellen was quaking in terror as she was led away in handcuffs, her freedom a thing of the past.

Yet a ten-year sentence isn't as hopeless as it first may appear. In my opinion, Guatemala is an enlightened, progressive country with a model penal code. What that means is that Mary Ellen would be eligible to have her ten-year sentence reduced to a mere two-year sentence—if she would agree to serve it in one of our state owned brothels. This is a generous provision of the penal code and I prayed she would accept it.

Probably the most widely publicized case of a convict electing to accept such a reduced sentence was that of Greta R. You may remember the case for those busybodies at Amnesty International put up a fuss. Fortunately, Guatemala ignores organizations that have nothing better to do than poke their noses into other peoples' business. Anyway, Greta was the attractive wife of a minor diplomat, from one of the new NATO countries, and she was arrested for drunk driving, having caused a three-car accident in which two people—excluding her—were injured. Drunk driving offenses are taken seriously in Guatemala and she was given a ten-year sentence at hard labor. After a week in the fields she was eager to exchange her ten-year sentence for two years in a brothel.

In her case, she was assigned to a brothel here in the capital. She was taught a couple of specialties and she became very popular. I can attest to that as I always found it necessary to phone days ahead to reserve her.

When Greta's sentence was up, to no one's surprise she asked to be allowed to remain in the brothel and her request was granted. She then became entitled to keep half her earnings and she has since made enough money to buy a lovely house on a beach near Champerico.

But not every girl had Greta's common sense. Unfortunately there were girls who took advantage of our generosity and then set out to escape, or at least try to escape. Something had to be done. Photos of the girls weren't the answer. In the brothels, the girls had ample opportunity to change the color of their hair, cut it or grow it long, and to otherwise alter their appearance. Guards along our borders, armed with photos taken at the women's arraignments, usually let these disguised escapees slip right through their fingers.

Fingerprinting was briefly considered. But it was learned that it took an expert to decipher the arches, whorls, inner and outer loops, the ridge minutia of the system.

Then one bureaucrat, a fellow who frequented the brothels, said, "Pussies are like fingerprints, no two are alike." It has been reported that when Archimedes discovered the principles of specific gravity, he shouted, eureka! And this was how we felt, no less pleased with ourselves than the Greek mathematician must have been. Pussyprints, could they be the answer?

The Guatemalan Academy of Sciences was convened. This august group of eleven men and one woman (whose orientation was always considered suspicious) spent a month in the brothels and returned with the unanimous conclusion that, yes, no two pussies are exactly alike, although "they exhibit remarkably similar features." Then this group was challenged with developing a moisture sensitive—as opposed to a light sensitive—variant of photographic paper. They were successful and all the girls were "printed." The prints were easily Xeroxed so a complete set—or "book"—was supplied to each border post. The system was almost infallible. A guard with a generous supply of moisture sensitive paper and a simple saw horse could "print" suspected escapees on the spot and either let them go on their way, if they were innocent, or return them to the justice system if their prints matched.

To facilitate retrieval, each book was divided into four distinct Pussy Types—four sections, if you will. They were: Vagina Grosera (plump), Vagina Falca (skinny), Vagina Ordinaria (ordinary), and Vagina Mordicativa (snapping). In that order. The last section is, by far, the smallest, but a border guard could always have hope.

So what happened to Mary Ellen, you ask? Well, she agreed to the reduced sentence.

It was early morning when she arrived at our building. As you may know a brass plaque by the entrance reads, EL ARAMIO DE LA SISTEMA PROSTITICION PENAL. She wore a gray prison dress of coarse cotton, and cheap hemp sandals. Her hands were red and cracked from the hard work. (A girl is never offered this opportunity until she has worked at least one week in the fields and, as in Mary Ellen's case, has calculated that that one long hard week was only 1/520th of her sentence.) Her long blond hair was matted and uncombed. She needed a bath. One could smell the sweat that had dried on her skin from the previous week's work. Her face was sunburned. She was tall so her skirt (made for the average 5'2" Guatemalan) fell well above her knees, accounting for the many scratches on her legs from the sugar cane plants. We were delighted she was joining our program for we feel it rehabilitates young girls, whereas the sugar cane fields only serve to increase their hostility toward society.

Her guard was in uniform and he wore the traditional Guatemalan tri-cornered hat. A rifle was slung over his shoulder. She was handcuffed to his left wrist. Since the door to the building had been locked after they entered, he removed the cuffs. He escorted her to a small office with a sign on the door reading, RECLUTAMIENTA. One of the men who worked in that office greeted her, but in Spanish, which she does not speak. He handed her a batch of documents that she was required to sign, and motioned for her to sit at a small table. An English-speaking co-worker entered the room and introduced himself as her translator since the documents were in Spanish.

I have witnessed this scene numerous times—these girls are never more desirable than they are at that moment, sitting there with a pen in their trembling hands. It is regrettable that they aren't in a position to appreciate the documents they are about to sign, for the documents are exquisitely written. Rather than the *lex scripta* concocted by lawyers, Guatemala turned to its poets as ones most suited to crafting such sensitive instruments. The documents turned out to be an inspiration to those of us who love Cervantes, Santayana, and all the great Spanish poets. For they describe in wondrous and lyrical detail what is required of our convict prostitutes. Who but a poet can understand the delicate bond between sex and servitude, pleasure and suffering? Mary Ellen's face had turned crimson—even on top of her sunburn—by the time the documents had been fully translated. Nevertheless, she began signing each page next to where it said "applicant."

Although our brothels pretty much have an "anything goes" policy, no activity is allowed that will physically harm any of the girls. (This was instituted after the Guatemalan Cavalry, just in from an unprecedented two months on maneuvers, cut a swatch through the brothels that has become a thing of legend.) Meals, lodging, medical benefits, a dental program, and crotchless panties are provided free of cost.

The last page to be signed required Mary Ellen to confirm that she was indeed of age. In Guatemala a girl has to be thirteen before she can legally work as a prostitute, and this is scrupulously adhered to.

Then she was given a small document, printed on glossy red paper, which has our official stamp. She could see that it had her name on it. She turned to the translator with a questioning look and he nodded and said, simply, "Why that is your license." He went on to explain that all prostitutes are licensed and are required to post their licenses "in a conspicuous place," much as grocers, taxi drivers, and other common laborers do.

Next, the guard led her down the hall to the "print" room where two men awaited her. The guard's boots were heavy on the ancient marble floors. The building is one of those Baroque colonial structures built in the 18th century but which have had little maintenance since then, I am sorry to say. The interior rooms haven't been painted for 100 years. They stopped at a door with a sign that read, EL SISTEMO RETRATO DE LA VAGINA. I followed them inside.

"Good day, Senorita," the senior of the two men said as Mary Ellen entered the room. "I speak English. I studied in your country." The man was new—I didn't know his name—but he had one of those Zapata mustaches the young rakes here are affecting these days. The second man, who was older, was simply a bureaucrat. Both were shorter than the American, even in her sandals. She handed the senior man her license and, with a flourish, he stamped it and gave it back. He said, "I recommend posting it above your bed, Senorita."

"Do you think they have any scotch tape there?" she replied.

"I'm sure they do. Now, there is just one more procedure before we can pronounce you an official Guatemalan prostitute."

"What is it?" she asked, uncertain. There is a saddle stand in the room and she must have thought it was out of place. The saddle sits next to tall windows that overlook a courtyard with classical statuary and old orange trees.

"We need to obtain a "print" of your vagina, Senorita, which will be used to identify you if you should attempt to escape."

"A whaaaaat?" She had a strong Texas accent.

"A 'print' of your vagina. Without which we cannot welcome you into the system."

"I'd go back to the fields? Y'all are saying that?"

"Faster than you can say, 'cheerleader.'"

She was close to tears. "Alright. But this is extremely difficult for me, hear?"

"Perhaps, but it is necessary." The man was unmoved.

"I mean, you wouldn't bull-eve the things I just agreed to do?"

"Then this part should be easy, Senorita."

"Ten hours of it everyday!"

"Why don't—"

"Perversions I have never heard of before!"

"First you must—"

"Anything the gentlemen want!"

"I really must insis—"

"On my back. On my knees. In my bum if that's what they ask for!"

"Please—"

"Ropes, handcuffs, paddles, dildos, whipped cream!"

"SENORITA!"

"Pardon? Oh, sorry."

"Senorita, you must co-operate." She nodded her head, yes. "Now, please," he continued, "I want you to part your hair." The man meant her pubic hair, and she understood.

"Does everyone have to be in the room?" she asked, defeated.

"Yes, as witnesses." Actually, the guard didn't have to be there but he had a gun, who was going to ask him to leave? "We will each sign the back of the print, making it official."

Reluctantly, she lifted her skirt and removed her panties in front of us. She reached down with one hand, held up her skirt with the other, and began parting her hair. She is blond down there and that, I'm not embarrassed to say, gave each of us an instant yet vigorous erection. She was untrimmed, which pleased me immensely. There would only be a short time in which to enjoy her luxuriance, for the older whores would eventually take her in hand and she would end up wanting to be trimmed into some sort of decorative design—Cupid's heart has become a popular choice in the brothels.

"Are you finished, Senorita?"

"Y-Yes," she said timidly.

"Then please mount the saddle."

The saddle is an English one of fine leather, as riding is an upper class sport in our country. The saddle fits over a custom made stand of polished wood, one that was made by a fine saddlery. On the saddle was a bluish sheet of paper.

"Like this?" she said, keeping her skirt at her waist. Since she needed one hand to hold up her skirt and one to hold onto the reins, she clenched her license between her teeth while she put her left foot in the stirrup and swung her right leg over and sat down on the paper.

"It will be ready in a snap," the man said. He had studied at MAC— Mississippi Agricultural College—and he is proud of his colloquial English.

Seconds later she was told she could dismount.

It was immediately obvious that the print wouldn't do. Numerous tufts of hair were in the way, making the print unacceptable.

"This time, please use a comb, Senorita." He went to his desk and returned with a comb and a hand mirror.

"I know I can get this right," she said, feeling all thumbs. "Maybe I need a chair?"

"Certainly." He rolled his desk chair to where she waited.

She sat down with her skirt bunched at her waist and examined herself in the mirror. "Well, I never! So this is what they look like?" she exclaimed, obviously never having examined herself before.

"Yes, but there are no two alike," the man said, proud of his knowledge. "They are like fingerprints."

"Well, I declare!" she responded. She needed to wet the comb. Seeing her pucker her lips and spit on the comb increased the intensity of our erections by two-fold, if that is possible. She parted her hair to either the left or right side, depending on how it grew. When she had finished she said so.

Once again she mounted the saddle and sat on a clean piece of paper. Seconds later she had produced an acceptable print.

We were astounded when we examined it! There was a general feeling of disbelief. Someone picked up the desk phone and, seconds later, men from other offices rushed in. Confused, Mary Ellen forgot to lower her skirt, which remained bunched at her waist. Her license was still clenched between her teeth—the men thought that was taking "post in a conspicuous place" to a new level of compliance. The sun streamed in through the windows, making her pubic hair look like it was spun of gold. The print was passed around, each of the men looking at it in awe.

Simply put, Mary Ellen had the prettiest pussy any of us had ever seen! This young, gawky ingenue from Texas had the prettiest pussy in Guatemala. Perhaps in the entire world?

We informed her of that fact. Some of the men shook her hand, others patted her on the back. One man begged to keep her panties as a souvenir. There were tears in her eyes but I took them to be tears of solace. I know our congratulatory display must have done a great deal to alleviate what would have been an otherwise humiliating experience for her.

THE PIMP WHO WAS TOO KIND

⁂

The girls took advantage of him—their pimp—never stopping to consider that he had a business to run. If he made some decisions that seemed hard to live with, well, so did the president of Pemex. Only you can bet the girls who work for Pemex don't get to flippantly disregard whatever rules they take exception to.

It was the bottom line—forgive the pun—the pimp had his eye on.

Take coffee breaks. The pimp decided a fifteen-minute break, every two hours, was adequate. Yet the girls took as many coffee breaks as they wanted, and business suffered for it. When he tried to enforce this seemingly reasonable rule the girls ignored him—until he beat two of them. The beatings were fairly benign, however. It didn't take the girls long to go back to their bad habits, for they knew they didn't have to take their pimp seriously if he was afraid to break a few bones.

He never attempted to regulate their potty breaks—although he certainly should have—for his girls used the *sanitarios* at the bus station like they were American tourists with the runs. The girls would sit in the stalls—but not with their panties at their knees as girls would do if they were truly answering nature's call. No, they would sit smoking cigarettes while customers searched the streets for more industrious whores.

His girls worked in Valladolid, which presented a particular problem—and that problem was the proximity to Cancun and Cozumel. American, French, and German tourists came to those places expecting to find whores who would do all the things they had only read about in certain paperback novels. They made demands that the girls believed were too extreme in nature. The pimp listened to their objections—for the girls had drawn up a list of twenty-five acts the men wanted them to perform but that they, the girls, objected to. After studying the list he ruled that they needn't perform five of them. In other words, the girls could say no to a full 20 percent of the extreme requests made of them. Is there a better definition of a kind pimp?

And the weather. It's too hot, was their constant complaint. To which he would answer, Does Pemex close down when it's too hot? Of course not. If that weren't enough, they would complain when their feet were tired. And he would respond, If your feet are tired, spend more time on your knees or your back. Sometimes a girl just needs to know someone is listening to her and that is what a kind pimp is willing to do.

Tips? What percentage of a girl's total earnings should accrue to her pimp? Most would agree it should be a full and complete 50/50 split—in other words, tips should be added to the pot and be split along with the rest of a girl's earnings. But he received less than his fair share for he was too kind—or too well mannered—to do more than a cursory search of their persons for the tips which they had most certainly secreted in places too delicate to mention.

Was the pimp rewarded for his kindness? Far from it. His girls constantly left him for other pimps. To find new ones he had to hang around the secretarial school in town looking for girls who were dissatisfied with their boyfriends, or with one thing or another, but usually just with the idea of sitting behind a desk all day.

When the secretarial school girls were taking a cigarette break—which they did outside on the sidewalk—he would engage one of them in a conversation. If it went well it would go like this:

"How are things going with you, chica?"

"Like shit, if you want to know."

"Well, maybe I can help you out?"

"How can a *stupido* like you help me?"

"You never know, do you? I've helped a lot of girls achieve their dreams."

"What dreams?"

"How much do you expect to earn as a secretary if they ever let you out of this place?"

"400 pesos a week, if it's any of your business."

"See, I can help you. How would you like to earn 5000 pesos a week?"

"5000? Doing what?"

"Just by being pretty."

"You are full of shit, do you know that?"

"I'm serious. Do you want to spend your life behind a desk? Taking orders from a boss with bad breath who pinches your ass whenever he wants to? Of course you don't."

"So?"

"Well, I may have something that will interest you."

"What would that be?"

"Do you like handsome men?"

"Yes but Tom Cruise is already taken."

"I'm glad you mentioned him. There was a man here last week who looked exactly like Tom Cruise. A girl ran off with him, which is why I have an opening."

"Are you serious?"

"Would you like to meet some handsome foreigners? To be very honest with you, they may not all be exactly like Tom Cruise. But they have a lot of money to spend."

"What are you leading up to?"

"Do you have a boyfriend?"

"Sort of."

"My advice would be to say goodbye to him. Many of those handsome foreigners are going to want to marry you. A boyfriend would only complicate things."

"Why would they be interested in me?"

"For one thing, because you are Mexican. It is known world wide that Mexican women are beautiful and desirable."

"We have big breasts and rears, that's all."

"Both of which add to your beauty. Never doubt that. And it's a fact there are a lot of lonely men in the world. They just want to meet pretty girls."

"I'm not so pretty."

"Are you kidding? You're gorgeous! I never kid about such things."

"My nose is too big."

"Who told you that? That's crazy!"

"Would you say my breasts or my rear is my best feature?"

"It's good that both are so pleasingly large. But it would be difficult to pick your best feature. I think maybe I like your eyes best, though."

"My eyes?"

"They are full of life."

"Really?"

"And your hair."

"But I haven't washed it in days."

"You're lucky to have hair that can look so good even if it isn't washed. You must use special conditioners?"

"No, just shampoo."

"Every girl should have hair like yours."

"Are there really rich men looking for girls like me?"

"Are you kidding? Of course there are."

"And you don't think I'm too fat?"

"Of course not."

"I weight 80 kilos."

"I would have guessed 60."

"Maybe I should diet?"

"Exercise. That's what you need. You need to be outside more."

"One last thing. Did you notice the mole on my cheek?"

"I haven't noticed it."

"It has a hair growing out of it."

"You know, a little make up will cover it. The other girls will show you how."

"You said 5000 pesos, right?"

"Sometimes more, sometimes less. What kind of work would you be doing if you stayed here?"

"Typing, mostly."

"That's boring."

"Know what I hate most about this school?"

"What?"

"They check each day to see if my nails are clean!"

"The men who will want to meet you won't care about things like that."

"No?"

"No. And if you miss a bath or two, who cares?"

"Wait! What about clothes? I don't have any money to buy new clothes."

"That's one of the advantages of this job. The fewer clothes you wear the better. Some of the girls don't even wear panties. They like their *chochos* to—"

"Watch your language!"

"Sorry, chica. I was just being enthusiastic about how casual we are."

"OK. But you haven't told me what you want me to do."

"Let's take one step at a time. First I want you to quit this school. Tell them you're never coming back."

"I have to do that first?"

"I have only one opening. There are many girls who would jump at the chance I'm offering."

"So after I quit, then what?"

"Then we go to step two."

"I have a pretty good idea of what you want me to do but I want to hear it from you."

"You haven't quit this school yet."

"I'm going to quit when I go back inside. So why not tell me now?"

"One step at a time, chica."

"It's something my family wouldn't approve of, right?"

"I voted for Vincente Fox and my family didn't approve. So how can I know what your family will do?"

"What if they kick me out of the house?"

"You will be able to afford a nice place of your own."

"I don't have much experience at this, you know?"

"Men will find that attractive."

"OK, I'm going inside to tell the manager. You know he won't give me my money back?"

"Tell him to stuff the money."

"Where will you be after I've said that?"

"Right here waiting for you. That's my car parked across the street."

Five minutes later she was back outside. "You better treat me good, you bastard."

She waited at the passenger's door until he understood that she wanted it opened for her. He walked around and let her in. Now he felt uneasy. She wasn't beautiful—although he had said she was—but she was spirited and obviously willing to take risks. She probably would find a rich foreigner to marry her. Then he'd be back where he was before.

DEATH BY MISS-ADVENTURE

✦

Yolanda and Sapphira, two whores from Nogales, didn't like each other. They argued constantly—arguments that might have escalated into bloody fights if they hadn't had the same pimp, a man named Nico. A whore with scratches on her face or a black eye was bad for business and Nico wouldn't tolerate it. He carried a pair of pliers, and Yolanda and Sapphira could imagine with great clarity how the pliers would feel clamped around their nipples—Nico's threatened mode of punishment if one of them misbehaved.

Nico was a short and dark Indian from Chiapas with an aquiline nose, merciless eyes and hard hands. The army had stationed him at Nogales, where he served his enlistment. He had expected to be stationed at the base at Cancun but the army surprised him. Most Chiapacos hate the army and avoid it but Nico had joined as a way out of the poverty he saw around him. Nogales wasn't Cancun, but he liked what he saw. He saw opportunity: if a man was a heartless bastard and had a couple of girls working for him he could make a living pandering to the Americans who crossed the border looking for fun. Nico had been born without a heart and girls were easy to come by.

Yolanda and Sapphira were Nogales girls and couldn't be mistaken for anything else. Both were pleasingly plump with big tits and asses, black eyes, red lips, a couple of tattoos each, and lots of hair. With short skirts, skimpy tops, stiletto heels and lack of underwear, a cigarette hanging from their lips, they were every American boy's dream of what a whore should be. They weren't girls to turn down a buck. If they had a motto, it would be: "Sure, sugar, I'll do that."

Oh, yes, they were also bi-lingually foul mouthed.

Nico and the girls sat at a table in one of the cantinas, watching television, since it was early and the businessmen and college boys from Tucson wouldn't drift in for an hour or so. The TV set hung over the bar and it was usually tuned to a sports program, as the Americans seemed to like that. At that moment there was a news program, on CNN, and one story caught their attention. A man in Germany—he seemed to own some sort of nightclub—had just offered $100,000 to any woman who could kill him by having sex. The man, who was briefly interviewed, appeared to be around seventy years old, so Nico could understand why he had chosen that rather pleasant way to exit life rather than waiting around for a heart attack or cancer. The German said he doubted there was such a woman but he held out hope the $100,000 enticement would prove him wrong. The report made the story into one of those humorous bits the stations liked to do so of course the two announcers were laughing as they related it. But Nico wasn't laughing.

"Did you hear that?" he said.

"That man in Germany?" Yolanda said.

"One hundred thousand dollars caught my attention," Sapphira replied.

"Think one of you could do that?"

"Fuck him to death?" Sapphira said. "Why not?"

"I bet I could fuck someone to death," Yolanda replied.

"With you, maybe he'd fall in and drown," Sapphira said.

"Let him eat your pussy, that would kill him quick enough," Yolanda answered.

"Shut up, you stupid whores," Nico said. "This is serious."

"The guy's in Germany," Yolanda said. "How does that help us?"

"I don't know yet, but I'm thinking."

"There must be plenty of girls in Germany who would want that money," Sapphira said.

"Yes, but they aren't Nogales whores," Nico replied.

"What do you mean by that?" they said in unison. It was difficult to offend them but it could be done.

"I think it would be a lot harder to kill someone that way than you think. But if anybody could do it, a Nogales whore could."

"I'm telling you, I could fuck a man to death," Yolanda said.

"Me, too," Sapphira added.

"The man wants to die," Nico said. "He's old. We should help him."

Both girls laughed and bucked their hips in imitation of fucking. The table shook.

"Chicas, you are thinking only with your cunts. This will take your intellectual faculties as well."

"Our what?" they said.

"Your brains, chicas. Use them."

"Why? Are we going to Germany?" Yolanda said.

"Just maybe I could afford to send one of you to Germany. Who knows?"

"You're kidding?" they said in unison.

"A trip there would be expensive. I'd have to be certain."

"Certain?"

"You would have to do it here first, as a test. Kill some poor bastard."

"No problem," Yolanda said. "The next man who comes along."

"I love Americans," Nico said. "I would hate to kill one. They are our fortune."

"There are millions of them," Sapphira said. "One won't be missed."

"The man might have a family. Does that bother you?"

"Want me to kill his family, too?" Yolanda said.

"Chicas, I think you have the right attitude for this."

"We are going to be rich!" they said in unison.

"Maybe," Nico said. "How would you go about it? Remember, use your brains."

Sapphira bent her head down past her waist and pulled her skirt up to briefly expose her pussy. "Hello, brain," she said. She started to laugh but Nico cuffed her on the side of her head.

"Shit, Nico! I was just kidding." She was angry but she thought for a moment. "OK, it would have to be an all-night fuck. An hour or two wouldn't do it or there would be dead men all over Nogales."

"Keep going," Nico said.

"You would have to keep him going for at least six hours. Maybe eight."

Yolanda joined in. "I'd keep my legs wrapped around his back so he couldn't get away—buck my hips to keep him moving."

"You can buck your hips for eight hours?"

"No problem."

"But no sucking," Sapphira said. "A blow job would allow him time to rest."

"If he wants to rest, insult his manhood," Yolanda said.

"Get on your hands and knees on the bed and make him fuck you from behind," Sapphira said. "Buck your ass back at him for an hour or so. Then get him back on top of you and keep your legs wrapped around him. Keep going back and forth between those positions."

Yolanda agreed. "You have to keep bucking and moving all the time so the man wants to keep up with you. Tell him he is giving you the best fuck you have ever had."

"But nonstop," Sapphira said. "The man can't have any rest."

"How do you do that? Men go soft," Nico said.

"The bartender sells Viagra," Sapphira said. Actually, the bartender supplied a whole pharmacy of drugs to Americans.

"You could put, like, a whole handful of them into his drink."

"I think it would be better to give him a couple of pills every hour." Nico said. "You would have to do the same thing to that German."

"No problem," the girls said. "Dissolve maybe 50 pills in a bottle of champagne. Keep the bottle next to the bed and keep handing it to him." This was the kind of expertise Nogales whores could draw upon.

"Chicas, I think you may be onto something here."

"Like maybe, one hundred thousand dollars?"

"Let's say the guy dies on top of you. Then what do you do?" Nico asked.

Sapphira answered. "I'd roll him off and phone you."

"No," Yolanda said, "I'd leave him on top of me. The police will need to see how he died so they don't ask too many questions. I'll keep my cell phone under the pillow."

"How long does it take before they begin to smell?" Sapphira said.

"Hours, chica, but I'll be there in a few minutes. Yolanda is right, keep him on top of you. Keep his cock inside you until the police get there. Remember, you are an innocent girl who is too sad and frightened to move."

"No problem."

Nico said, "The unfortunate accident will get into the papers, then we can send the article to the German."

"I'll put a note with the article, 'You're next, sugar!'" Sapphira said.

"No!" Yolanda snapped. "I'm going to be the girl in that article."

"Chicas, I'm only going to take one of you to Germany. One of you has to prove to me you can do it. The first one who does, we go to Germany. Split the money, fifty-fifty."

"The next man who comes along, hasta la vista, baby!" Sapphira said.

"Wait a minute, not many men want to pay for a whole night," Yolanda said.

"You girls are offering a 'special' tonight," Nico said. "One hundred dollars to enjoy your young bodies for the next eight hours."

"Shit!" the girls said.

"This is a small sacrifice. Think of the reward, chicas. I may go back to San Cristobal and buy a ranch!"

"You better take us with you. Who's going to do all that work?" They broke out laughing.

"Chicas, I'm not afraid of hard work."

"Sure," they said.

As the cantina began to fill up, Nico went to the bar to buy some Viagra and to keep out of the girls' way. They remained at the table, waiting for the right men to come along. The strip clubs in Nogales were busier—often filled with men—but Nico felt the men who went to them were there to drink and look. Men who came to the cantina had only one thing on their minds. Actually, both girls had been strippers before Nico began running them. They liked this better—they had been turning tricks anyway—but they no longer had to listen to drunken cat-calls regarding their, well—amplitude.

A few men came in but other girls left with them. It was thirty minutes before two men approached the girls. The men wore running clothes, of some sort, and Nikes—not the usual clothing the girls saw. The men seemed to be willing—even eager—but when the girls said they were only interested in an all-nighter, the men declined, stating they had to be at a meeting back in Tucson early in the morning.

"They looked fit," Yolanda said after the men had left.

"Athletes, maybe?" Sapphira answered.

"Any second thoughts?" Yolanda asked.

"No." Both girls secretly believed they could send an eighteen-year old decathlon gold medal winner to his grave if they wanted to. But why take a chance? "Maybe Nico's right. Older men might be better?"

"A man with a heart condition would be better."

"How are you going to know that?" Sapphira said.

"I'll ask," Yolanda answered.

"Be subtle about it then."

"What do you know about subtle, you dumb whore."

"Who are you calling a whore, you whore!"

"Careful, Nico is watching us."

"He knows less about being subtle than you do."

The girls dismissed a few college boys who stopped at their table. Sapphira said, "I'd like to kill one of those fuckers." Yolanda agreed.

They were the reason why the two girls carried cell phones. The college boys' idea of fun was to have a couple of buddies with them in the room, while the girl had to service all of them at one time. That paid well but it sometimes got out of hand, especially if the boys had been drinking. There was only so much a girl could do when three erections plus six hands were fighting for her full attention. The phones were programmed to quick dial Nico, and Nico was formidable with a baseball bat.

Then two likely candidates came into the cantina. Nico had told them to pick two men who resembled the German—older men—as they would make the best guinea pigs. These men were younger, probably only in their forties, but the girls liked them, as they looked less fit than the others. The men wore sport clothes but they had obviously left their suits back in a hotel in Tucson. Yolanda and Sapphira sized them up as being married—they had that look—and the girls were never mistaken about that. They probably had plenty of money but Nico had been firm: "Keep it simple, he had said. You girls aren't interested in money all that much, you just want to make love." "What's that?" they had answered, laughing. "Remember when you were twelve? It's what you thought you were doing with your boyfriends while they were fucking you. Now, ask for only one hundred dollars but make sure the men are willing to stay all night." When the men noticed Yolanda and Sapphira, the girls slowly crossed their legs, making it plain they had somehow forgotten to wear panties. That brought the men hustling over to their table.

"Join us for a drink?" Sapphira said.

The men sat down. "What are you two lovely girls up to?" one of the men asked. He told her his name was Donald.

"Waiting for you, sugar," Sapphira answered. She had just put on lipstick and she made kissing motions.

"Actually, we're looking for men who are macho enough to keep a girl company all night," Yolanda added. She didn't want to waste any time on them if all they wanted was a quick fuck.

"Really? That must be expensive?"

"Not for the right men." Yolanda placed her hand on the arm of the man who had not yet spoken or given his name, claiming him.

"No?" Donald said.

"If I thought a man could love me all night I'd go with him for one hundred dollars," Sapphira said.

"You're kidding?"

"I'm a girl who needs love, Senor." She moved her chair next to Donald's, so that their legs were touching.

"Me, too," Yolanda said. "I need love."

"Tim and I could use some serious loving," Donald said. "That's one hundred dollars for the whole night?"

"A small tip would be nice. But only if we deserve it." Yolanda lowered her eyes as if what she had just said embarrassed her.

"You're on!"

"You can stay all night?" the girls said in unison. "Like, until noon tomorrow if we want?"

"You bet!"

"Sapphira, we may have found the right men," Yolanda said.

"May?" Donald said.

"We're particular," Yolanda said. "May I ask a few questions?"

"Like what?"

"Have you had any unusual weight gain or loss in the last six months?"

"I've put on a few pounds?" Donald said.

"Any shortness of breath?"

"Sometimes?" Tim said. This question confused him as much as it did Donald.

"Have to get up frequently in the night to urinate?"

"Sure."

"Sure."

"Loss of appetite? High blood pressure?"

"I suppose so . . ." Tim said.

"Double vision? Hearing loss?"

"How did you know?" Donald said.

"Any cough or cold that persists?"

"Maybe?" Tim said.

"Wait a minute?" Donald said. "What is this?"

"Just kidding around," Yolanda said. "We'd love to go with you!"

"Well, then, since that's settled, what are you drinking?" the one named Tim said.

"Champagne!" the girls said.

"Good idea!" He called to the bartender, "Four glasses of champagne, *por favor*."

"Let me get them," Yolanda said, jumping up. When she came back from the bar two of the glasses had Viagra dissolved in them.

They touched glasses in a toast. "Here's to two beautiful women,"

Donald said. "Hear! Hear!" Tim added. The men received kisses on their cheeks. They were pleased that the girls seemed so genuinely interested in them.

"I know you aren't going to believe this," Donald said. "But Tim didn't want to come here."

"No?" Yolanda said.

"I thought it might be dangerous down here," Tim said sheepishly.

"Oh, Tim," Yolanda said, "what could happen to a strong man like you?"

"Well, you hear stories."

The men agreed that they would each buy a bottle of champagne to take with them to the girls' rooms. They did this shortly after Sapphira had put her hand on Donald's crotch and Yolanda had pulled Tim's zipper down and slipped her hand inside.

Yolanda had made a quick decision when she chose Tim: he weighed less than Donald. The police might take up to an hour to get to her room and the less dead weight on her all that time the better. She knew Sapphira had wanted Donald because he was overweight, and overweight men are prone to heart attacks. Yolanda thought that had made Donald tempting. Yet she figured that Sapphira would be sorry, that Sapphira hadn't considered what his dead weight would feel like on top of her all that time. Actually, what she really believed was that she would get the job done and Sapphira would just end up with a hundred dollars and a sore pussy.

"Are Mexican girls always this friendly?" Tim asked.

"Yes," Yolanda said. "We are brought up that way."

"I can't wait to see you without clothes," Donald said to Sapphira.

"Here?" she said, joking.

Donald laughed. "*A su casa*, baby."

"Then let's go," she answered.

Nico watched them leave the cantina—the girls taking the men to separate rooms. He had slipped the extra Viagra pills to the girls while the men were settling the bar bill. Now all he could do was wait. He turned on his phone.

"Do we need a taxi?" Tim asked Yolanda.

"No, sugar, my room is close by." They began walking.

Yolanda remembered the scene from *High Plains Drifter*—her favorite movie—when Clint Eastwood passes by an undertaker on his way to a gunfight. The undertaker is hammering a coffin together. Clint doesn't say a word but he holds up three fingers, signaling to the man to begin building coffins for the three men waiting for him up the street. She wanted to be able to hold up one finger—as silently as Clint had. One of Nogales' undertakers did come into the cantina once in a while. What were the odds of seeing him that night? The odds were small but, miraculously, as she and Tim walked toward her room, there the man was, coming toward them! As they passed him, Yolanda held up one finger.

The undertaker saw the gesture. *High Plains Drifter* just happened to be his favorite move, too. He immediately understood the significance of her raised finger. Without saying a word, he turned around to walk back to this work room to begin constructing a coffin.

When the call came in to the police station the captain said, "We have a dead American in a whore's room. Probably a heart attack."

The captain and two of his deputies arrived at Yolanda's room and saw that there was a nude man lying on top of her, not moving and a little green in color. Nico stood off to the side, not wanting to get involved.

The captain laughed, "Chica, what happened?"

"Get him off me and I will tell you!"

"Oh, no, chica, we need to photograph this." He gestured to one of the deputies who left to get a photographer. "You can wait another thirty minutes."

"Shit!" Yolanda said.

"Who is this man?"

"His name is Tim. I met him last night."

"In the cantina?"

"Yes."

"He approached you?"

"Yes, I was just sitting there with my girlfriend."

"Strangers in the night, eh?"

"Yes."

"How long were you and the man together?"

"A few hours."

"A few hours? Like how many?" He picked up the champagne bottle to examine it. It was almost empty.

"Maybe six or seven, who remembers?"

"Interesting."

"He insisted on staying all night."

Then the captain bent down to examine the dead body. "He seems to still have an erection? But of course you must know that."

"Why do I have to wait like this until a photographer arrives?"

"The Americans will want proof of what happened. Don't you think?"

"Shit."

He laughed. "Sorry, you won't be able to put on lipstick and comb your hair."

"Don't photograph my face!"

"We want the Americans to see how lovely you are. It will explain why the man must have been so tempted. Yes, we will photograph your face. Also, the German may wish to see it?"

"What?"

"I saw an interesting news program on American television last night. There is a German who has offered one hundred thousand dollars to a girl who can kill him through sex."

"I didn't see the program."

"That's too bad, since you appear to be well qualified to earn the reward."

"Oh?"

"I think you did see the program? If you did and this poor dead American was a test run, then it might be construed as murder?"

"Oh, shit."

"I need to get back to the cantina," Nico said. "You will excuse me?"

"Yes, get out of here, Nico," the captain said. Then he asked the remaining deputy to move out to the hallway. "Guard the door," he said.

"Now, chica, we are alone and free to talk."

"This fucker is getting heavy."

"Only ten or fifteen more minutes. Before the photographer gets here we have to come to an agreement."

"Like what?"

"How to split the one hundred thousand dollars."

"Nico was going to give me fifty percent."

"But Nico can't charge you with murder."

"Shit."

"You are certain you can kill that German?"

"Yes, easily."

"Then I'm thinking a 60/40 split?"

"What about Nico?"

"I don't think Nico needs to come with us, do you? Have you been to Germany before?"

"No, of course not."

"Castles along the Rhine. The Berlin botanical gardens. The—"

"I think Tim is beginning to smell!"

"You are right, he is, but I hear the photographer coming now. Do you want any prints for yourself? Perhaps a few enlargements to send to your relatives?"

When the photographer and the deputy came in, the photographer recognized Yolanda and said, "Yolanda, how nice to see you."

"Carlos, just take your pictures, OK? No small talk."

"But I saw your cousin last week. She said to say hello."

"Carlos, can't you see that I have a dead man on top of me?"

"Of course I can see that. That's why I'm here. Did you know your cousin has a job at that new plant the Americans built? She told me she likes it very much. She also said you never call her."

"I will call her next week. Now, please, Carlos, take your pictures!"

"The lighting is terrible in here. You should buy some lamps."

"Captain, can you help me?" Yolanda said.

"What do I know about lamps?" he laughed.

The photographer placed his camera on a tripod, took a reading with a light meter, fiddled with the aperture, then began taking pictures. "Yolanda," he said, "do you think your cousin likes me?"

"How should I know?"

"Should I ask her to go to the movies?"

"If you don't finish I'm going to smash your camera!"

"OK! OK! But try to smile."

The deputy, who had returned with the photographer, had been trying unsuccessfully to get the captain's attention. Finally, he took the man by the sleeve and pulled him aside. Then he whispered, "Captain, there was a message for you at the station. There is a second American dead in a whore's room."

"Another American?"

"Yes."

"What's the whore's name?"

"I don't know, sir."

The Captain had a sickening thought. The color drained from his face. He turned to Yolanda. "Where's Sapphira?"

"Hopefully at the pharmacy buying liniment," she answered.

"Please tell me Tim didn't have a friend!!!"

"Well . . ."

Now the Captain thought: Two of them! The American press will investigate and find out what happened. The Governor will be breathing down my neck . . . Germany would have been so lovely this time of the year.

THE SECRET LIFE OF WALTAMITA

At the crack of dawn they took Waltamita from her dank prison cell out to the walled court yard. There were bruises on her arms and legs where she had been beaten. Yet there were no bruises about her head, as you might expect there would be. The soldiers—as brutal as they were—were incapable of striking such a perfect face. She squinted from the sun, for she had been held in the dark for weeks, yet her eyes—as those close enough to observe her would later testify—were large and brilliant. Hadn't Colonel Roberto Alma-Sanchez told her a thousand times that they were the most beautiful eyes he had ever seen?

Six men were lined up in the center of the court yard, leaning on their rifles. Her firing squad. They wore ill-fitting uniforms that were stained from sweat and dirt. She could see they were mere boys, conscripts certainly. They lowered their eyes in shame when she looked at them. There was no shade in the court yard. While the temperature would rise to 100 by noon, Waltamita's body would soon cool to the temperature of a shallow grave.

A general in full uniform approached her. "You know where Roberto is," he said matter of factly. "Give him up and you will live."

"I love him," she answered.

The general knew that was all she would ever say. If she hadn't broken when they beat her she wouldn't now. Nevertheless, he tried one last time. "Your colonel is a traitor. We will find him soon enough and what will it have benefited anyone that you lost your life?" When she said nothing he continued "We know the information you gathered at the brothel from our, shall we say, loose-lipped officers went to Roberto. Yet we will forgive your spying if you decide to talk." She remained silent. "Yes, no doubt Roberto thinks he loves you, too? But even if he succeeded in overthrowing the government, do you think he would allow you, a whore, to share the palace with him?"

"I love him," she answered again.

"Yes, perhaps he would make you our First Lady?" The general laughed at that—our first Lady, a former whore! "But, no matter, Senorita, for I must carry out your death sentence." At that point a captain stepped forward and led her to the wall—which was pocked with bullet holes from past executions—and began tying her arms behind her.

"Do you want the blindfold?" the captain asked, after he had finished tying her arms. He held the cloth up to her.

"No," Waltamita answered.

The captain rarely saw such bravery. Most men welcomed the sense of safety, however false, the blindfold provided.

"A last cigarette?" he asked.

"Yes, please."

He put the cigarette in his own mouth and lit it. Since her hands were tied behind her, he placed it between her lips and let her take a deep drag before removing it.

"Thank you," she said.

"*Vaya con dios*," he said, stepping back. A priest attempted to give her the last rites but she laughed at him. The captain saluted her and the firing squad raised its rifles. He took his sword from its scabbard and lifted it above his head. When he lowered it the men fired. The villagers could hear the poppety crack poppety crack sounds the rifles made . . .

Just then a car, which was stopped at the curb, honked at Waltamita. "Hey, are you asleep or something?" the driver said.

"Sorry," she answered. "Do you want a date, sugar?"

"You looked prettier from a distance," the man said.

She leaned into the open window so her breasts would tempt him. "I'm not so bad, am I?" she replied.

"Well, you'll do, I suppose. But you definitely aren't young. Been out here a few years?" he said.

"Who's counting?" she answered.

"I thought so. Your tits sag. It's a dead giveaway."

"Hey, just touch them! They're as firm as melons!"

"Maybe I should look for someone else."

"Come on, you'll like me," she said.

"Forget it if you think I'm going to pay a lot."

"What do you like to do?"

"Anything frighten you?"

"No. And I can be reasonable."

"You mean, cheap?"

"Whatever."

"That's what I like to hear."

"Want to do it in the car?"

"No, is there a hotel around here?"

"A couple of blocks away," she said.

"Get in then."

An hour later, Waltamita walked back from the hotel. She had a cut lip which she dabbed with a handkerchief as she walked. He had been rougher than she expected. Besides her lip, she would have plenty of bruises tomorrow. Not only had the man not given her a tip but he had refused to give her a ride back to her corner.

It would have been easier walking if she weren't wearing four inch heels, which hurt her feet. She took them off and walked barefoot. The soles of her feet were soon black, but her thick calluses prevented her feet from being cut from the debris that littered the street.

. . . She had just arrived back, and was putting on her shoes, when a large limousine pulled up to the curb and slammed on its brakes. A chauffeur quickly opened the rear door and Dr. Raul Garcia-Lorca de la Madrid, the most famous surgeon in the country, got out.

"Why, you're as beautiful as they say," he said, looking at her. "Thank God you weren't with one of your customers. We have only an hour in which to save either the Queen or the Princess! Without a kidney transplant neither of them will last another hour!"

"How can I help?" Waltamita said. She noticed the chauffeur was weeping.

"Tests have shown that you are the only person in the country who is capable of being a kidney donor for one of them. We believe it is only fair that the decision as to which one lives—our beloved Queen or her lovely daughter the Princess—be left up to you, Waltamita." Hearing that, the chauffeur began crying openly.

Waltamita didn't hesitate. "I know a way that both of them can be saved," she said, calmly but resolutely...

"OK, let's have the money," her pimp said.

"What?" She was momentarily confused. She hadn't seen him walk up.

"The money! All of it! Now!"

She gave him the money her rough customer had paid her.

"Is this all you got?"

"It's all he would go for."

"I don't know why I bother with you."

"My regular should be by. He pays more."

"For fuck's sake then, put some lipstick on that cut. Do you think the guy is going to want you bleeding all over him?"

She rummaged through her purse for her lipstick. "That last one was a bit rough."

"You know what I told you about complaining?"

"I wasn't complaining. Just stating a fact."

"Yeh, well, I got things to do. Be back in an hour," he said.

. . . She was glad he was gone. Tom Pitt, probably the most successful CIA operative in Latin America, was also glad he was gone. He had been watching Waltamita for days. Now he crossed the street to where she stood. He needed her help—he had an offer he desperately hoped she wouldn't refuse . . .

THE SOAP COMPANY PRESIDENT'S DAUGHTERS

It was a daring contest for a company to stage. Nevertheless, a well-known soap company announced a contest to select a whore who would become the company's spokesperson for a year. That was just the first step. An advertising campaign was designed around the soap's purported ability to successfully launder anything, even a whore's panties. The company—assisted by said spokesperson/whore's panties—was determined to prove its claim once and for all. A new slogan— "If we can make hers bright and clean as new, think what we can do for yours!"—was designed particularly to appeal to Mexican women who had begun buying competitive American soap brands. Although the Mexican soap powder was a first-rate cleaning product (due to the high borax and lye content) American companies had been gaining market share. There are some fifty million women in Mexico and estimates are that 80 percent of them wear panties. The demographics were excellent.

Actually, the campaign and the slogan had been thought up by the two bored and spoiled daughters of the soap company's president, for they were clever girls no matter what else they were. At first, their father questioned the campaign's appropriateness but he finally decided it would make the company appear broadminded and democratic. Later, public opinion would confirm his judgment.

All a girl had to do was buy the soap powder, clip the coupon on the side of the box and mail it in, then wait to learn if her coupon was the lucky one that was drawn. This was the soap powder Amaranta normally used to do her laundry so buying a new box was no big deal, although she didn't need more soap and she did watch her money carefully. She followed the instructions printed next to the coupon and went to the post office the next day on her way to work.

The two bored and spoiled daughters knew that few actual whores would respond to the contest but that thousands upon thousands of ordinary girls would send in their names on the chance of winning. Who would ever know whether they turned a few tricks on the side? The daughters also knew that few of those girls would bother to read the small print.

Amaranta was a waitress.

She was among the 80 percent who wore panties.

You can imagine how surprised she was a few months later when she received a special delivery letter informing her she had won! Yes, won! She had to sign for the letter, which she did with her hand shaking, as it was the first important letter she had received in her life. The letter included traveling expenses and a bus ticket to the capitol, where she was to present herself at TV Azteca a few days later, where, in prime time, she would be introduced as this year's spokesperson!

Amaranta remembered a radio program, from when she was a little girl, called "Queen for a Day." Her mother had desperately wanted to win . . . For the lucky woman got to take the day off from work and she would be given prizes such as a trip to a beauty parlor. But this was bigger. This was the soap company's spokesperson for a year! And it paid a lot—well, she didn't know exactly how much, for she hadn't read the small print.

She managed to get a week's leave from her job at the VIP restaurant in Merida. She was a hard worker and the manager wanted her back. She left a note—with one of the other waitresses at the restaurant—to be given to her fiancé, should he ever come around. She hadn't seen him in weeks and even his own mother had no idea where he was. Amaranta had phoned his mother looking for him. His mother had said he wasn't worth it, that she should find someone else. She agreed with her—he wasn't worth it—but having a fiancé who didn't want to get married was better than having no fiancé at all. She knew if he would set a date she would marry him. When it was slow at the restaurant she would sometimes get a coke and take a seat at one of the empty tables. She had memorized the marriage ceremony and, as she sat there, she would imagine the priest saying, *The woman, whose principal attributes are abnegation, beauty, compassion, perspicacity and tenderness, should and will give her husband obedience, pleasure, assistance, consolidation and counsel, always treating him with the veneration due to the person that supports and defends her.*

She walked to the bus station. It was still early morning and it was cool enough to walk while carrying her suitcase. She liked Merida well enough but she didn't feel at home there. Like half the population of the city she had come from one of the smaller towns in the state looking for work. If she were walking to the restaurant she would have a bag of food scraps with her that she had gathered the day before so she could feed the hungry dogs along the way. She couldn't understand how people could be so indifferent to the hunger they saw among their animals. A tourist at the restaurant—who had seen her gathering scraps—told her that animals were well fed in the States. But she treated that information as just another of the fantastic things she had heard about that country, none of which could possibly be true.

She arrived early at the station so she could get a seat on the bus by the window, as she had never been far from Merida and she wanted to see what all of Mexico looked like. When the bus pulled out it was nearly full. They drove for hours along the Gulf of Mexico, passing through Campeche, which she saw had more forest than the Yucatan, then as the bus passed through Tobasco she was surprised at how wet it was there, and yet they still hadn't come that far. The oil refineries in Veracruz were ugly and fouled the landscape and she and the other passengers feared the rest of Mexico might be like that. But as the bus entered the beautiful valley where the Federal District lay, their spirits lifted. Even the smog she could see in the distance hovering over the city couldn't mask the beauty of mountains taller than she had ever imagined.

Many of the passengers had been with her since Merida and they had gotten to know each other. The bus had changed drivers but each driver was friendly and had talked with them. Everyone wished him good luck when his shift was finished and he relinquished the bus to another driver. She hadn't told anyone about her good fortune for it would have seemed too much like bragging. There had been one young man on the bus who had complimented her every chance he got. "Your dress is lovely. Did you get it in Merida?" "I like the style of your hair. It's so modern." She was secretly pleased with the compliments—he was so handsome—but she reminded herself that she had a fiancé.

The bus had stopped for food and it had been easy to sleep in her seat with the back reclined, but there had been no opportunity to wash except for her hands and face at the bus station restrooms when the bus stopped. The trip took two days and then some.

She arrived in Mexico City just in time to make it to the TV Azteca studios without being late. She had to take a taxi from the bus station and was surprised at how much of her money that took. (The two daugh- ters of the soap company president had carefully calculated what it would take to get from Merida to the studios and had planned on Amaranta arriving broke.) She brought her suitcase with her as she didn't have time—or the money—to rent a room where she might leave it and, hopefully, change her dress and freshen up. She had worn her best dress for the trip—as the young man had noticed—and now it looked solied and wrinkled.

When she told the guard at the door who she was, he immediately summoned another guard, who took her to the studio where they would be broadcasting. The host shook her hand and told her he was delighted to meet her. He was someone she recognized—Fernando del Solar or Carlos Torres, she thought, but she couldn't remember which one as she had been too excited and confused to catch his name.

"Chica, we must get you dressed. We go on the air in twenty minutes!"

"I have clothes in my suitcase," she said.

"Chica, the soap company has provided you with new clothing."

The host's assistant—a young woman with large *chichis*—took her to a dressing room and handed her the outfit the two sisters had personally chosen for her. When she arrived back on stage she was wearing a fake-leather mini-skirt, a halter top of a thin satin material in a leopard print, fishnet hose and four-inch stiletto heels in which she could barely walk. The assistant had teased Amaranta's hair so that it was full and provocative and she had painted Amaranta's mouth with crimson lipstick.

She was momentarily blinded by strobe flashes from cameras that began taking pictures for tomorrow's editions of the newspapers. Finally, the auditorium lights were dimmed and the TV cameras were turned on. The host put on a big smile. They were on the air.

He greeted the audience and explained that the event was not only being televised, but was being run on radio stations throughout Mexico. He thanked the president of the soap company for giving "a young whore" the chance to represent his company for a year. She would undoubtedly become, he said, "one of Mexico's newest bright stars!" With that announcement the studio audience cheered and the photographers took more pictures. Amaranta was so excited she almost fainted.

The host told her, "a representative from the soap company will pick up your panties"—that brought a titter from the studio audience—"each week, and they will be photographed, in glorious color! Next they will be laundered before being photographed again. Then, Amaranta, the 'before' and 'after' pictures of your panties will be used in extensive print and TV advertising!" Then he told her what her prize money was and that astonished her for she had never conceived of it as being such a large sum. (The two sisters had personally insisted on that sum to insure the winner had no second thoughts.)

"In fact, here's your check!" He gave it to her and, with a shaking hand, she put it in her skirt pocket. "Now," he continued, "I know our audience would like to know more about you!" The studio audience cheered. "Where do you ply your trade, Amaranta?"

"Merida," she said timidly. She hadn't expected to be asked any questions.

"Is the city as beautiful as they say?"

"Si, it is quite beautiful."

"Of course you only get to see it at night?" That brought on studio laughter.

She did work the night shift at the VIP restaurant. "Si, I work at night. But sometimes, if there are a lot of tourists in town, I also work the day shift."

"Wow, two shifts?"

"Si. The other girls do it, too."

"You girls are real troopers! But, don't your . . . you-know-what's get tired?" The audience roared with laughter.

She thought he meant their feet. "Si, sometimes we go in the back-room and soak them in a pan of hot water."

"Well, that leads to my next question. Just how many men per week get to enjoy your company?"

She tried to think fast. She served dinner to about twenty-five men per night. Times seven, that would be 175 men. No, she couldn't possibly use that number. She had never even met a whore but even she knew 175 would be too high. What about seventy-five? That sounded better to her but she wasn't sure. "Seventy-five?" she said. When the studio audience cheered she felt she had picked the right number.

"Wow!" the host said. "The soap company has the right girl!"

"Thank you," she replied.

"Now, you must meet men from a lot of countries?"

"Si." The VIP restaurant was a tourist favorite.

"Which do you like best—Mexican or American men?"

"American men?" A moan from the audience.

"And what is the main difference between the two?"

"American men leave bigger tips." Laughter from the audience.

"How big a tip does a pretty girl like you get?"

A meal at the restaurant was about 100 pesos. An average tip was 15 pesos. "Fifteen pesos?" she said.

"A dollar and fifty cents?"

"Si."

"What do you do to earn that 15 pesos tip? Remember, now, we're on television!"

"I tell them what the 'specials' are."

"Go on . . ."

"I make sure what I serve them is hot."

"Go on . . ."

"I clean up their mess after them."

"And all for a dollar and fifty cents!" More laughter from the audience. "Well, it's been good talking to you, Amaranta. But now, I have a surprise!"

"Si?"

"Si. The soap company doesn't want you to return to Merida."

"No?"

"No. They want you to be in the thick of the action! A hotel room has been rented for you in Tijuana! For a year! Compliments of the soap company!"

"What?"

"A pimp is waiting for you in the alley in his Trans Am and he is going to drive you to Tijuana where you, Amaranta, will be given the best corner in town!" Loud applause. "And, there's a bonus! The *USS Yorktown* has just docked in San Diego and 500 sailors are now heading for Tijuana!"

Terribly confused—but caught up in the wild applause—she allowed two guards to lead her down the back steps to where the pimp waited. He was idling his engine and banging his fist against the dash in an attempt to get the air-conditioning to work.

The soap company president's daughters were rolling on the floor with laughter in front of their large TV set when Amaranta was taken away. They hadn't counted on the *USS Yorktown* being in San Diego but they thought that was a good touch. They weren't at all fooled by Amaranta. They guessed she was a maid or a waitress or something

– 114 –

like that. Actually, they envied her somewhat. Whoring was probably the only job the two girls would have wanted for themselves if they actually had to get a job. Well, maybe being a Hollywood movie star would be OK. They could play fiery, jealous, voluptuous Mexicans with bad tempers as well as anyone. But that would mean getting up early to be on the set so who needed it? One of them thought being an astronaut would be cool but the other one reminded her that they would have to wear silly space suits rather than designer clothes so that job was also out.

In the excitement, Amaranta had left her suitcase and purse in the dressing room. But she was still too confused to worry about things like that. She wanted to ask the pimp to drive her back to Merida but she had taken the check and that would mean cheating the soap company. What to do?

She got in beside the pimp—who was named Julio—and the Trans Am laid down three feet of rubber heading for the circuito interior, then the Pacific Coast Highway. The Trans Am needed a valve job but it could still do 120 miles per hour, a speed the pimp had every intention of reaching. The soap company had alerted the federal highway patrol so the car could travel without fear of being stopped for speeding. For, as Julio well knew, the *USS Yorktown* sailors had been at sea for six months and had a lot of back pay to spend. He wanted to get her to her corner before the other whores had picked the sailors like chickens.

"Better give me that check," Julio said. "We'll have a lot of expenses to cover. You can sign it over to me later."

Uncertain, she took the check from her pocket and gave it to him. "Will you drive me to Merida?" she said.

"Merida? Are you kidding?"

"I have to get back to my job . . ."

"I'm driving you to your job. Those sailors are horny."

"But—"

"Let me see your tits, chica." They had only driven a few blocks.

"Si?"

"Now, *pour favor.*"

"Why?" she said. There were tears in her eyes.

"I need to decide what you're worth."

She pulled her top down exposing two firm, plump breasts.

"Now your pussy," he said.

She hesitated but then she pulled her skirt up to her waist and slipped her panties down to her knees.

"Those are old ladies' panties. I will get you some tiny ones that make you look sexy. Give those to me."

She slipped them down her legs and over her heels. She handed them to him and he flipped them out the open window. But she kept her legs together.

"Chica, why are you sitting there with your legs clamped together tighter than a *pata de mula* clam?"

She lowered her eyes and didn't answer him.

"If your legs are not always open and inviting, some men might say, 'that girl must be a waitress, not a Tijuana whore,' and they will look elsewhere to spend their money. Do you understand what I'm saying?"

She remained silent.

"Whores must not know much in Merida," he said.

She still could not bring herself to answer him.

"For example, do you know how to bitch and nag until your john agrees to pay a much higher price than he wants to?"

"No. . ."

"Do you know how to look over his shoulder to read his PIN number if he has to use an ATM machine?"

"No. . ."

"That number can be very useful to us. I was listening to the broadcast on the car radio. Do you know what a Tijuana whore would do to a man who left only a dollar and fifty-cent tip? I'll tell you. She would kick him in the balls! I'll teach you how to do that. With pointed toe high heels it hurts like hell."

"Si?"

"Do you know how to quickly go through a man's wallet while he is cleaning up in the hotel bathroom—without leaving fingerprints?"

"No..."

"I can see that you have a lot to learn. But don't worry, a few months from now you'll know everything there is to know."

"What if I can't learn everything in a few months?"

"Chica, you must think positive. That's the key to life. Did you leave a boyfriend behind?"

"Si . . ."

"He will be jealous of your success."

"Si?"

"You are a TV star, Amaranta. You are going to be famous. Rich gringos will come across the border just to spend an hour with you."

"Si?"

"But none of that seventy-five men per week stuff. The girls in Tijuana work much harder than that. Now, spread your legs so I can get a look at you."

She spread them as far as the seat would allow.

"Ah, chica, you are *muy fina*," he said.

Amaranta did become famous. Julio got her some very tiny panties and that first year she gave the ones she wore to the representative from the soap company when he came for them every week. "Before" and "after" pictures appeared on TV commercials, billboards, and in print ads. In the TV commercial, technicians in white lab coats were seen taking the freshly laundered panties from the washer and holding them up so the camera could zoom in for a close-up. The campaign was so successful that a number of American soap brands beat a hasty retreat back across the border.

As predicted, rich gringos did come just to spend an hour with her. And many were the sailors who returned to sea with her picture taped inside their lockers. A couple of times the soap company president's daughters traveled to Tijuana where they disguised themselves as teenage boys before picking her up. Her fiancé tried to contact her but she had lost interest in him. As for *pata de mula* clams, well, it was said that the only time her legs were together was when she was sleeping— if then? Eventually, the mayor of Tijuana named a street after her— *Calle Amaranta*. It runs off *Avenida de Revolution* and it has some of the finest shade trees in town.

As for the soap company president's daughters, they were lured to New York with promises of an abundance of money by Sachi & Sachi, one of the world's largest advertising agencies. The girls now spend their days sitting in boring "creative meetings" and dreaming of returning to Mexico.

THE PRACTICAL WIVES

Buying back husbands isn't easy.

It isn't easy even when the whore who has them can't wait to be rid of them.

Nonetheless, five of the most prominent wives in town did manage it. Of course, it cost them a pretty penny.

These aren't the sort of wives who go to the night table to see if the revolver is there, tempting as that may be. No, they're wives who open a bottle of Chardonnay and fill five glasses and sit down together to talk things over. A few oaths, a few tears, but there are no bullets that need to be dislodged from their husbands. Do we want the *bastardos* back? After venting a little steam, of course the wives do. How much are they worth to us? Estimates range from a few pesos to a more considered calculation of the value of the annual shopping trips to Dallas and Miami the husbands provide. Still, are there any good alternatives we can pursue? And so on. Love? Heavens, no, the word is never mentioned.

This debate took place at the mayor's house while he was at work—he had no idea it was taking place and, worse, that it was his fate, along with the other husbands, that was being decided. Finally his wife, the chief of police's wife, the banker's wife, the doctor's wife, and the factory owner's wife, decided to pay up. You might wonder why they didn't just say good riddance, and go on with their lives. Indeed, the idea crossed their minds.

But they are practical women. Women of their class are bred to be practical and they hone the skill once they are married.

I was there during the debate although I wasn't asked for my opinion. (I had a juicy one but I kept it to myself.) They had hired me to negotiate with the whore because—due to my proclivity for my own sex—they felt they could trust me not to fall under her charms.

The husbands knew nothing about this. They were a miserable lot but, of course, they would have attempted to thwart my actions, for their misery came about not because they were in thrall to the whore but because each one was forced to share her with the others.

Although no longer young, the wives are still attractive women with good legs and firm breasts (or, more likely, firm bras). Yes, perhaps their rear ends have grown a trifle too broad. Yet I've heard heterosexual men can like that. The factory owner's wife is the most attractive of the five, but in a cheap, tarty sort of way (OK, so I'm jealous), and the banker's wife is still pretty enough to turn heads. Attractiveness isn't enough, however—husbands like a little diversity in their sex lives.

The whore in question had arrived in town only a few weeks earlier.

After my first meeting with her I reported back that she wanted 50,000 pesos—per husband—to release the men. I say "release them" but that has to be considered in context. They functioned reasonably normally at their respective jobs—but that was at the whore's insistence, for they wanted nothing more than to be with her, to serve her, to share her bed. They went home only to change clothes. Fifty thousand pesos seemed an intolerable amount to the wives, and the women naturally wondered if their husbands would regain their sanity on their own.

"Have you seen the man who is with the whore?" I asked.

"The man who seems to be her servant?" He had been seen around town shopping and doing errands for her. When they were together he walked two paces behind her.

"Yes. It seems several women in Campeche also paid to get their husbands back. He was one of the husbands—I believe he was a lawyer—but she decided to keep him for her own amusement."

"He stays with her?" the banker's wife said.

"I don't believe he has any choice."

"How long has this been?"

"Two years, I believe. Before she took him he was a well respected man in Campeche."

"But he appears to be nothing more than her slave," the factory owner's wife said.

"Exactly."

"So the only hope we have is to pay?" the mayor's wife said.

"I believe so."

"Will she be reasonable?"

"I believe she knows she has the upper hand."

"She must be extremely beautiful. Otherwise how could she pull this off?" the police chief's wife asked.

"Not exactly beautiful—but earthy, the way some whores are."

"Young then?"

"Closer to your ages," I answered. This surprised the wives, who hadn't seen her, and didn't want to.

"Did she try to tempt you?" the mayor's wife asked.

"Yes, as you expected she would. She said she had a small scratch and asked me if I would give her my opinion as to whether or not she should seek medical attention. As soon as I said I would she lifted her skirt and removed her panties."

"No!"

"Yes. She then took me by the hand and led me to her bed. She lay back and spread her legs and explained the scratch was next to her— well, you know the area I'm referring to."

"We call them pussies," The doctor's wife said amid much laughter.

"So that's what they're called!" More laughter.

"Raul, what would you do if you had a pussy?"

"I'd enslave your husbands," I replied.

"Oh, you are nasty! But apparently you would have to stand in line." The mayor's wife was impatient. "But—you didn't?" she said.

"I examined her only."

"Would you have done it with her—for us, I mean—if she had demanded it?"

"Yes, if I thought it would help. I would close my eyes and think of Antonio Bandaras."

"I close my eyes with my husband and think of him myself," the factory owner's wife said, and they all laughed.

"Ladies, please!" the mayor's wife said. "Now, Raul, please continue. Was there a scratch?"

"Yes, there was a scratch of some sort—perhaps left by one of your husbands?"

"Don't be catty."

"I told her it was nothing to be concerned about—"

"I bet it was my husband! He scratches me sometimes . . ." the chief of police's wife said, without thinking. "My God, did I just say that?"

"Yes, but we would prefer not knowing," the others said, trying to suppress their laughter.

"Tell us, was she different down there?" the banker's wife asked. All of them believed there had to be a simple explanation for their husbands' behavior.

"Well, she was completely shaved," I said. "I assume that isn't commonplace?"

"Oh, my, no!" Pause. "What does it look like when a woman is shaved?"

"Very much like a sea shell, would be my description."

"Would a man like that?"

"Ask your husbands."

"But there must be more to her than that? How can she enslave all these men?" the mayor's wife asked.

"To learn that, Senoras, you would have to be a man and make love to her." (What I didn't tell them was that the whore had given their husbands permanent erections and they needed to make love to her at least once every eight hours or the pain of the erection would become unbearable. I didn't relate this information as I had no reason to be cruel to my employers.)

"What did she think of your resistance to her?"

"She was confused at first. But she finally understood. That's when I left to convey her demand for 50,000 pesos."

"Go back to her and tell her we will pay 25,000 pesos and no more," the mayor's wife continued. The others agreed.

I returned to the whore with a counter offer of 25,000 pesos.

The whore laughed. "Tell them I'm considering a duel. Yes, the husbands will fight a series of duels over me—the reward for the last one alive will be to permanently share my bed."

"Would they kill for you, Senorita?"

"Come and examine that scratch more carefully and decide for yourself."

"No. I'm inclined to believe you."

I reported her threat back to the wives. It was at that point they weighed what they would inherit from a husband killed dueling, against years of his future earnings.

"My husband is good with a pistol," said the wife of the chief of police. "I hope he doesn't shoot everyone."

"If he did, he would be arrested for murder," I said. "Dueling is against the law."

"Alright, 35,000 pesos!" They agreed to the larger sum.

"Now I'm angry," the whore said after I returned with their latest offer. "Yet I will accept 35,000 pesos—but on one condition. If that condition isn't accepted immediately then I will leave today and take all five men with me." Then she whispered the condition to me.

When I returned to the wives, I told them she had accepted their last offer.

"You've done well, Raul!" the mayor's wife said.

"I'm afraid there is more."

"A condition?"

"Yes. A condition you must accept immediately, as she has threatened to leave town and take your husbands with her."

No inheritance. No future earnings. Resigned, they said, "Alright, we have no choice but to accept, we can see that. But what is the condition?"

"You are each to write your name on a piece of paper. I'm to put the paper in a hat and draw out one of your names."

"What?" the five said in unison.

"Whosoever has her name drawn is required to shave her pussy, then return with me—along with the pesos—to the house the whore is renting. Oh, yes, I'm to bring a lock of the shaved hair with me."

Clearly distraught, they implored me to go back and tell the whore they would accept her original demand of 50,000 pesos.

"I'm afraid it will do no good," I said. "I truly believe she will leave if you don't comply."

"But what can we do?" the doctor's wife asked.

"Write your names on a piece of paper," I said.

Trembling, each wife wrote her name and handed the paper to me. I placed them in a hat I borrowed from a hall closet, reached into it, and chose one. On it was written, Mercedes. She was the banker's wife. She immediately fainted.

"Grab her, girls!" The other four women took advantage of her condition and quickly carried her into one of the bathrooms where they shaved her before she woke up.

When they returned with her she was fully dressed but by the expression on her face I knew she was as bald as a baby under her panties.

"We should go," I said.

"I'm naked!" the unlucky wife said.

"Mercedes, don't be stupid. You're wearing a dress, slip, and panties," the mayor's wife answered.

"Why do I have to do this?"

"I'm sure she just wants to humiliate one of us."

"She's done that."

"Now take this money and go with Raul." Mercedes was handed a very smart little purse stuffed with cash. The mayor's wife slipped me the lock of hair. "We'll make our husbands pay for this, Mercedes. When they take us to Miami shopping you'll forget all about this."

"If I go outside like this every man will know!"

"How can they?"

"Raul knows!"

"Raul is one of us."

"More or less," I agreed.

"Mercedes, Raul will bring you back here in twenty minutes. Won't you, Raul?" the doctor's wife said.

"Absolutely."

Mercedes and I walked to my car. She was shaking so uncontrollably that I had to put my arm around her waist to keep her from falling.

I felt guilty. There was more to choosing her name than I had just admitted to. For some reason Mercedes had chosen to write her name on a piece of yellow paper while the other wives had chosen white. I hadn't watched as they wrote their names so, at that point, I didn't know which of them had chosen yellow. I was determined to be impartial but I was irresistibly drawn to that bright spot of color. From the angle at which I held the hat, it was possible to select it without my doing so being noticed. Yet I reached for one of the white pieces, determined to let the yellow one lie. But at the last moment, well, you know what happened.

We arrived at the whore's house and she welcomed us inside. From the living room we couldn't help but notice the bathroom door was open. The lawyer from Campeche was on his knees scrubbing the toilet. The desperation on his face turned my blood cold. The whore pulled the door closed so we wouldn't be distracted.

Mercedes was still shaking as she handed over the purse. Then the whore lifted Mercedes' skirt and slip, pulling them up to her waist, which exposed pale pink panties that were transparent enough to reveal that the frightened wife had indeed been shaved. The whore stroked one finger across Mercedes' mound and said, "Did they have to tie you up to do this?" Mercedes didn't answer but she made no attempt to flee. After a minute the whore let the slip and skirt slide back down. "Cat got your tongue?"

"I fainted," Mercedes said meekly. "That's when they did it."

The whore laughed.

Mercedes cried.

I thought about the lawyer scrubbing the toilet.

"Let me count the money," the whore said. After she was satisfied it was all there she picked up an urn and removed five locks of hair.

"Are those—" I started to ask. (I recognize that kind of curly hair when I see it.)

"They are," she responded.

She smiled at me and with two fingers, imitated the action of a pair of scissors, letting me know she had gathered the locks herself. She placed the locks on a table, waved her hands over them, mumbled some nonsensical words and said the men were released from her power.

As for Mercedes—well, that's another story. First, let me say that the whore explained that earning a living on her back was tiring work. There weren't that many men who were worth enslaving, so most of her days were spent doing old-fashioned whoring. Having a partner to service half of her customers is an idea she had been toying with for some time. "You can't imagine how many overweight men there are," she said.

"Yes, I can," I replied.

"I need someone to relieve me of part of the load—forgive the pun."

I thought—oh, oh!

She turned to admire Mercedes. "You chose well, Raul, thank you. You may go now."

"And Mercedes?" I said, although I knew the answer.

"She stays with me."

Mercedes finally understood what was happening. "Oh, God, no!" she said.

"I promised to return with Mercedes," I said defiantly.

"Don't test me!" the whore snapped back.

"I can't do it . . ." Mercedes said weakly.

"You can and you will."

I tried to act, well, like a man. "You can't—"

"She wrote her name on a piece of yellow paper—"

I was taken aback. How could she know? "How could—"

"Did you think, *mericon*, I had no power over you?"

"But?"

"How would you like to be married to a fat wife and have five children? I could make that happen."

"No . . ."

"Then give me the lock of hair—and leave now. Without Mercedes."

"I'll pay you anything you want if you let me leave with Raul," Mercedes said, her voice was quaking.

"No, it isn't just money. I'm tired of working on my back all day."

"But I've never liked sex! Ask my husband!"

"All you have to do is lie there and smile. No one will ask you if you like it."

"For God's sake, Raul, please help me!"

"I can't make that ten children, Raul. Muchos diapers to change."

I started to take Mercedes by the arm but the whore said, "Your wife will demand that you perform oral sex, Raul. Every night." There was terror in Mercedes' eyes but no less in mine. "I'm sorry," I said, releasing Mercedes arm. I handed over the lock of hair.

"Now, let me see how nice you look without clothes," the whore said. She began unbuttoning Mercedes' dress. I slipped out the door.

The whore bought a car with the ransom money and a chauffeur's hat for the lawyer from Campeche. The three of them left town that same day.

The banker made no attempt to locate his wife. He had recently hired a new secretary and she was able to console him on his loss. I wasn't tempted to search for her myself, for the thought of having a fat wife and ten children was more than enough to keep me at home. The other four husbands agreed to take their wives shopping in Miami. The wives asked me to join them but I wasn't up for it. "We'll do all the clothing stores, jewelry stores, and art galleries!" I made a feeble joke about not liking to do that much walking in heels.

Of course the four wives have been dying to know how Mercedes is getting along. (Their own lives aren't as much improved as they had hoped they would be.) Most of their speculation has centered around how many men Mercedes services a week and whether the men are handsome or not. Then, a man who had seen Mercedes—she was working out of a bar in one of the towns along the Costa Maya— reported back that she is having the time of her life. She discovered she likes sex after all.

So, you just never know.

MARY ELLEN RIDES AGAIN

⁂

The time came when Mary Ellen faced a choice. She had been in the Guatemalan brothel system for two years, the full length of her sentence. (This is one penal system where there is no time off for bad behavior.) Anyway, the choice she faced was: remain in Guatemala and go on to enjoy a long and lucrative career on the new pillow-top mattresses that had just been installed in the better brothels, or leave the country as she was now free to do.

She chose to leave.

What? Where is this story going? Well, her motives aren't as clear as they might first appear. She held no grudge against the Guatemalan judicial system, and the pillow-top mattresses were admittedly a major upgrade. She had no interest in returning to college in Texas. She might have returned if the Anthropology Department of the University of Texas had offered her a full professorship. She felt—in the years she had spent in the brothel—that she had earned the equivalent of a PhD in male studies. But the department at Texas declined, stating budgetary constraints. Or so the letter said when it arrived during the last week she was at the brothel. Yet that was all for the better, she thought, for she had developed a romantic interest in a Mexican business man who had become a regular customer. He had told her to look him up if she ever got to Mexico City.

Her superiors had done their best to convince her to stay. While she wasn't the best young whore they had ever trained, she managed to retain a naivete that made her popular with a certain segment of the clientele. Of course, as a "free whore" she would have more control over the things the brothel required her to do. Nothing would have given her more pleasure than being able to gather up all the paddles, dildos, ropes and so forth that cluttered her room, and throw them into the dustbin. But she left them for the next girl. As she was leaving her room for the last time she did turn to give the pillory that stood in the corner—it had holes for a girl's head and hands—a big kick. Since the pillory was solid wood she barely scuffed it, but kicking it gave her some satisfaction.

Reluctantly, an official from El Aramio de la Sistema Prostiticion Penal drove her to the Mexican border, which she crossed on foot.

She had no money. Not a peso. But she was wearing one of those skimpy little dresses the brothel provides for the girls and her long blond hair was radiant, for it had been brushed three hundred strokes the night before by a fetishist who had hired her just for that purpose. She carried a small suitcase that contained the rest of her dresses, a modest amount of underwear, plus the cutest little strappy heels.

A pick-up truck was about to pass by so she stuck out her thumb indicating she wanted a ride. The driver slammed on the brakes.

The driver told her he was going to San Cristobal. That's a good start, she thought. He asked her if she had any money and when she said she didn't, he offered to take her there if he could have thirty minutes with her in the back of the truck.

That request didn't surprise her one bit and, since it wasn't much different from what she had been doing the past two years anyway, she agreed. The driver pulled off the road, where they could have some privacy, and Mary Ellen climbed into the back of the truck, lay down on some sacks of cacao beans and pulled her skirt up to her waist.

She gave the driver the best thirty minutes of his life.

She didn't own a watch but she had developed an internal clock that told her exactly when thirty minutes—or an hour—was up. In the last two years she had said, "That's all you get, senor," more times than she could remember. Time is every man's enemy but never more so than in a brothel.

The driver was an older man who owned nothing but a dog and the broken down truck that was taking them to San Cristobal. Years of squinting into the sun as he drove had weakened his eyesight but he could still see well enough to know that what he had just had, he would never see the likes of again. Even his dog, which had curled up on the floor of the cab at Mary Ellen's feet licking her toes, understood that.

The driver was missing a few teeth, his hair and mustache had long been gray, and his face was deeply creased, but Mary Ellen could see he had once been handsome. She referred to him as *mi camionero guapo*, which pleased him a great deal. When he learned she was going to the capital, he was tempted to take her himself—just for the pleasure of being able to look at her—but he knew his old truck would never get that far.

They drove through rain and cloud forests before ascending into the Sierra Madres, mountains so rugged and high it was possible to see the Pacific Ocean out the driver's window and the Gulf of Mexico out her own. They passed through a cool valley and then came into San Cristobal, a city of colonial buildings and remarkable light.

She was let out at a truck stop and the driver went on to unload the sacks of beans that had been their temporary bed. It didn't take her long to find a truck that was going to Tuxtla Gutierrez.

No sooner had she jumped into the second truck when the driver asked her if she had any money. When she said she didn't, he agreed to take her if she would give him thirty minutes in the back of the truck. This time she was smart enough to ask for a sandwich and a coke as well.

They climbed into the back of the pick-up and she saw they would have to lie on the hard surface, as the truck bed was empty. The truck bed was also dirty, so she shed her dress rather than just pulling the skirt up to her waist. He gave her his shirt to put under her but it wasn't much cleaner than the truck itself. In spite of these hardships she still gave him the best thirty minutes of his life.

Once they got on the road the man confessed he was married. His eyes were flooded with tears as he said it. "That's, OK," she replied, "I haven't done it with anyone who is single since my ex-boyfriend and I hitchhiked to Costa Brava. Bring your wife some flowers when you get home." The man was slightly comic-looking anyway, and with tears in his eyes he was pitiful.

A little while later he stopped the truck after she spotted a bed of wildflowers growing along the roadside. He asked her to forgive him for the bargain he had made her accept for her ride. *This man shouldn't be a truck driver*, she thought. She was tempted to lie down among the flowers and pull him down on top of her to show him she felt no resentment. Instead, she felt the best thing to do was to help him pick a bouquet, large enough to hopefully convince his wife of his faithfulness.

The landscape continued to be beautiful. They stopped to look at the Sumidero Canyon, which was so deep the Grijalua River, maybe a thousand feet down, looked cool and inviting rather than green and full of snakes, its true self.

They arrived in Tuxtla Gutierrez and she was let out at another truck stop. It was dinnertime and she was hungry. She found a truck that was going to Juchitan in the morning and the driver agreed to let her sleep in the cab overnight, and ride with him the next day if, of course, she would first give him thirty minutes in the back of the truck.

The truck was carrying boxes of something or other and they pushed them aside to make room for two bodies. Up went her skirt and he let out a loud gasp. *Que mono!* You have the prettiest pussy a man has ever seen, he said. So I've been told, she replied. She then proceeded to give the man the best thirty minutes he had ever had in his life. He was so pleased he bought her dinner.

Over a dinner of chalupa *coleta tortillas,* he told her a sad story. He had only been out of jail for six months. Five years earlier he had shot his wife who had been cheating on him. His wife survived the gunshot but he had gone to prison. Now he couldn't find her or his child, a son of about seven. One of the reasons he had taken this job was that being in that cell had made him want to see more of the world. She understood how he felt.

He said he hadn't smiled or laughed in five years. But seeing Mary Ellen sitting across the table from him—her skin still flush from sex—made him realize life was worth living.

They arrived in Juchitan the next day about noon. She had loved hearing his stories about prison life and she had told him hilarious tales about things that had happened to her at the brothel. He wanted to marry her—he told her he would never shoot her even if she cheated on him. I swear it, he said, I would shoot myself before I'd shoot you. She declined his offer, as gently as she could.

At the truck stop she had no difficulty finding another truck, this one going to Oaxaca. The driver asked her if she had any money and when she said she didn't, he told her he would take her if she would give him thirty minutes in the back of the truck.

She said, OK, but throw in lunch. So another truck driver received the best thirty minutes of his life.

The driver carried an old coke bottle filled with *palque,* an alcohol made from cactus, and they took turns drinking from it. He had tattoos on his arms, chest, and back—she had seen them close up when she earned her ride—and he asked her permission to allow him to have a heart tattooed with her name on it. She said she would be honored. Where should I put it? he said. She found a nice spot up high on his right arm where she traced an imaginary heart with her finger. He asked her to write her name on a scrap of paper so he wouldn't forget how to spell it.

They came upon shepherds with flocks of sheep that stubbornly refused to let them pass. But she was in no hurry and wouldn't let him lean on the truck's horn. When the truck started to overheat he stopped by a river to get water. There were some women washing their clothes and they were friendly so she took the opportunity to wash her dress— she had worn it and slept in it for three days. She also took a bath and when the driver stopped to watch her, the women told the driver that was bad manners. But he ignored them. Later, she tied the dress to the truck's aerial so the wind would dry it as they drove along.

In Oaxaca she found a truck going to Acatian. The driver asked her if she had any money and when she said she didn't, he told her he would take her if she would give him thirty minutes in the back of the truck. The truck had a lot of old furniture in the back and it also had an old mattress, which allowed her to more fully utilize some of the tricks she had learned.

She showed the man the best thirty minutes of his life.

The driver was a handsome man who seemed to know it. I do this in the truck with women all the time, he said. He told her he was delivering the furniture to his nephew, who had just gotten married, but he was now considering if he should keep the mattress. She asked him if he had used a mattress with the other women he had had in the truck. He said, of course not. So she told him to give the mattress to his nephew since he had done well enough without it and, besides, the two of them would have had a good time anyway.

The landscape had changed. It was less rugged and there were more farms, although the farms seemed small to her compared to the ones in Texas. They passed 2000-year-old cypress trees, 100 feet high, considered the oldest living things on earth.

In Acatian, she met a truck driver who was going to Cuautla. He asked her if she had any money and when she said she didn't he said he'd take her, plus he would share his lunch, if she would give him thirty minutes in the back of his truck. She ate lunch first—tamales stuffed with chicken, prunes, almonds, and chilies—then climbed into the back of the truck.

There, she gave him the best thirty minutes of his life. And she did it, believe it or not, on a stack of lumber. You could do this for a living, he told her.

The driver was a *Mestizo*—but mostly Indian—and he had a good singing voice. He sang love songs all the way to Cuautla. Most of them had sad endings but one, in which the lovers got together after much travail, he agreed to teach her. They sang it as a duet two or three times before she got it just right.

Her Spanish had become fluent after two years in Guatemala so she was inspired to make up a song for him. It was about a girl who got splinters—you know where, since her lover screwed her on a bed of lumber—but she decided not to pull them out as they were a sign of honor. He laughed and sang it to the tune of *Ti-Pi-Ti-Pi-Tin*. Later, when he dropped her off at a truck stop, he was still singing her song as he drove away to deliver the lumber to a construction site.

In Cuautla, she had little trouble finding a driver who was going to Mexico City the next day. He told her he would take her, buy her dinner, and let her sleep overnight in the cab if she would give him thirty minutes in the back of the truck. She said, I'll make it an hour if you also throw in breakfast tomorrow.

He readily agreed and she gave him the best hour of his life.

He didn't do badly by her, either, for he had once been a prizefighter and he still had a strong back, fluid hips, and the stamina that the ring required. He had the most glorious body she had ever seen and she had seen a lot of bodies the past two years. Of course, most of the brothel customers had been flabby. Worse, they wore strong cologne, which she disliked. This man smelled of sweat and hard work.

The driver would have been a perfect specimen except that he had only one eye. He had been mismatched in his last fight and he had been beaten badly. Having only one eye disturbed his sense of distance perception and he came close, a dozen times, to running into the vehicle in front of them while Mary Ellen held onto the dash fearing the worst. Let me drive, she said. Can you drive a truck? he said. Yes, she answered, plus I've got two eyes. OK, he said, you drive, but if my hands aren't on the steering wheel, I can't guarantee where they'll be.

He continued to drive and they arrived at the outskirts of the city without incident. But the landscape had turned depressingly urban. The poverty she saw looked bleak, it wasn't the manageable poverty she had seen in the rural areas. There were too many cars, and smog obscured any sun that might have lifted her spirits.

He was going into the city to pick up some canned goods to bring back to a market in Cuautla, so he asked her where she wanted to be dropped off. She was suddenly unsure, as she was having second thoughts about this city, but mostly about the businessman in whom she had been romantically interested,. She compared him to the unshaven, unwashed truck drivers she had met and he didn't come off well. The businessman had worn dark suits and now suddenly, worn-out blue jeans looked good to her.

More importantly, she hadn't seen much of Mexico when she had traveled with that prick of an ex-boyfriend. They had been too interested in marijuana, reading Cormac McCarthy novels, and feeling each other up, to be good tourists. Now, having traveled by truck the last few days, she had seen Mexico as she hadn't seen it before. For the last two years, in the brothel, she had seen little more than the ceiling of her room or the sheets on her bed when a customer flipped her over onto her stomach. Now she wanted to see everything she could. She momentarily regretted not marrying the ex-convict and traveling with him.

I've changed my mind, she said. Drop me off at a truck stop. You don't want to see Mexico City? he said. No, I think I'll maybe head up into the Yucatan, she replied. After that, who knows?

Why not stay with me a while? he said. You married? she asked. I was. She left me when I lost my eye. She smiled, I'm more interested in what you have in your pants, she said. Yes, but that's got one eye, too, he answered, also smiling. Sure, it's supposed to, she said.

Myths are rife in Mexico. . But that doesn't mean some of them aren't true. Over the last few years numerous people—many of them respectable witnesses—have sighted a blond gringa who travels by truck throughout Mexico. She is sometimes called *La furgoneta guera* in the songs that are being written about her. It is said that being with her cures melancholy, epilepsy, malarial fever, and impotence. On the other hand, it has also been said that being with her causes melancholy, epilepsy, malarial fever and, at some later inopportune time, impotence—but that may just be the result of comparing her to a current lover.

A team from the Instituto Mexicano de Cinematografia set out to film a documentary, to settle this contradiction once and for all, but the team returned three months later empty handed as they been unable to locate her. She has been seen as far as Baja California to the north, along the gulf from Tampico to Telchac Puerto, and, for some reason, especially along the Oaxaca coast. Of course, if all the sightings were true she would have to have been in two or three places at one time.

Descriptions of her differ slightly but they all agree that she wears skimpy dresses, has blond hair a man could lose his soul in, and has no money with which to pay for rides.

ONE SMALL STEP

❧

Alessandra—Lexie to those who tune in mornings at nine—is a TV journalist. That means she is one of those girls in revealing clothes you see bending forward, tits aimed at the camera so that they might share their abundance with you—no selfish girls in this crowd—all the while delivering the titillating stories their industry confuses with news. Since Lexie is less endowed than most of her female colleagues the camera, under normal circumstances, would find it difficult to peek down her top. That is, it would if she didn't compensate. Lexie has learned to lean even further forward, far past the 45 degree angle which is the standard for her profession. That's hard on the back and hard on the feet. Who said journalism is easy?

One day, while reading through stacks of newspapers for ideas that she could develop into stories for her TV audience, a small article caught her attention. She learned that a man had been smothered. Not unusual in itself, people are smothered all the time and nobody cares, but apparently this guy got his head stuck under someone's left tit. Lexie thought, She has to be a girl of record dimensions, right? To add some more color, the girl works in a brothel in some God forsaken Yucatan village. Now there's a story worth being on TV!

Lexie took a moment to daydream. She wondered what it would be like to have lethal tits. She could picture her jerk of a boss backing away from her, his face expressing terror—what a delicious image!—as he screams, don't point them at me—they're killers!

If only she weren't terrified of surgery. If she had bigger tits she would be doing prime time. Almost all of the other girls have "gone under the knife," as they humorously describe this fourth estate career move. Some of them have silicone tits so perfect they won't bounce unless the girls are running and they cross the twenty miles per hour threshold (as they often have to do to be first at the scene of an accident).

As it is with the rest of the world, Mexican journalism has succumbed to being little more than a search for sex and scandal and celebrities. It's no longer the goal of our journalists to merely find fault with a president's policies—who cares about policies? What is he doing in his bed? Preferably in beds other than his own. An apparently corrupt governor of the State of Louisiana once said, I'll be reelected unless I'm found in bed with a live boy or a dead girl. He was right, for he knew that details of his financial corruption were commonplace, it was not what the world wanted to know. Journalists everywhere have rushed to take up challenges of this sort—for wasn't the governor challenging us? Governor's and president's beds have never been more closely scrutinized. Yes, Manuel Buendia, our late journalist extraordinario, must be spinning in his grave.

Anyway, back to death by mammillation. Yes, this was a story all of Mexico would soon be talking about. Carmelitia's fifteen minutes of fame. But, with any luck, Lexie would get four times that amount. In a fickle world like we live in, an hour of fame isn't anything to sneeze at. Of course, the notoriety would probably ruin Carmelita's life, but that was her tough luck. Perhaps, Lexie should say, that's entertainment?

Lexie told her boss what she was up to and he said, "You mean she killed some poor bastard that way?"

"That's what I'm going to find out," Lexie answered.

She booked a flight from Mexico City to Merida where she rented a car. She had only been in the Yucatan once before and that was to spend a weekend in Cancun. How different this part of the peninsula was. Raw but beautiful. She came across towns with strange Indian names: Yaxkukul, Cansahab, Buctzotz. Yet she zipped right through them without slowing down for none of her viewers would be interested in stories about Indians unless Carmelita's tits had just sent one of them to the happy hunting ground. She passed groups of Indians along the road side. They waited, stocially, for busses that, as far as she could see, never came. The gravel that kicked up from her tires caused them to quickly gather their children and turn their backs to the road to avoid being pelted in the face. She was at the brothel in less than two hours.

The brothel was in a fine old building on a tree lined street. She parked in front then checked her purse to see that she had her notebook and her digital camera. Once inside she marched into the *putanero's* office like she owned the place. She immediately began her spiel. Had the *putanero* been paying closer attention, instead of mentally undressing her, he would have learned all he would ever want to know about such topics as the public's right to know, the role of a free press in society, and Lexie's willingness to go to jail before revealing her sources, "Just like that girl from the *New York Times*."

Over the years the *putanero* had grown hard of hearing and that, coupled with the fact that he had mentally removed every stitch of her clothing, and was now imagining how she would look bent over his desk, meant he hadn't understood a word she said. He assumed she wanted a job so he offered her one. Although he was hard of hearing, he wasn't blind.

"Turn around," he said. Amused, she did what he asked—did he just offer me a job? "You have a very fine ass. I predict you will be very popular."

Lexie had the whorish beauty that's a requisite for all Mexican female TV personalities. No doubt the *putanero* had noticed her lavish make-up. And he couldn't help but notice her long hair that had been bleached to where it was as blond as a Hollywood star's. (He only owned an old Phillips radio so how could he know that there are more blondes fighting for air time on Mexican television than there are blondes in Copenhagen? Make that Copenhagen, Oslo, and Reykjavik.) Plus, she wore the traditional TV personality's skin tight Capri pants, a halter that covered as best it could but, give it a break, it was just a strip of fabric, what do you expect, and high heel sandals that made a lot of noise and allowed her painted toenails to shine like rubies. In truth, the *putanero* could be forgiven for misinterpreting her profession.

"Yes, yes, I need a job," she said. She had sized him up by now and was sure he wouldn't let her near Carmelita once he understood she was a reporter. She wanted to be free to roam about the brothel until she found the young but resourceful murderess. "Let me get my luggage from the car."

"We're short on girls tonight," the *putanero* said. "Go into the parlor. I'll have someone bring your luggage up to your room."

She found the parlor. There were four girls talking to about a dozen men. Although they were big girls, no doubt about that, she was disappointed that none of them actually had tits large enough to have smothered anyone. Theirs were sixes, maybe sevens, on the M.S.H. (Mexican Standard Handful) Scale—far from being lethal. So, Carmelita couldn't be among them? Oh, well, no story worth its salt comes easy. . . . But, speaking of tits—which in her job she was often forced to—she could see she certainly didn't stack up well compared to these girls.

One of the men approached her and for a moment she thought he was her cameraman from the station. He wasn't, of course, but he did look a lot like him and this momentarily confused her which allowed her conditioned reflexes to take over. She bent forward. Starring down into her cleavage, the man was pleased by what he assumed was a very nice come-on and it clenched the choice he had to make. Of all the girls there, he wanted Lexie.

Once she determined the man wasn't her cameraman she returned to an upright position but by then the man had slipped his arm around her waist. Then he tried unsuccessfully to slip his free hand down inside her Capri pants. This was meant to be just a friendly let's-get-to-know-each-other gesture. If he had known her true profession, he would have instinctively known that TV journalists wear pants that are so tight that panties, forget hands, can barely fit inside them, and he wouldn't have wasted his time.

With the man's arm still around her waist, they headed upstairs to her room. She hadn't wanted to go with him and she considered pushing him down the stairs. It was not that she was still confusing him with her cameraman, although that was part of it. OK, so she had gone to bed with her cameraman. That didn't make her a whore. Not when you consider that much of Mexican "news" consists of interviewing other TV personalities, movie stars, singers, and other entertainers—and who wants someone else's tits getting most of the air time? She needed a cameraman who was willing to let his camera linger on the right parts of her anatomy, not her guest's. Too bad you just spent 10,000 pesos on new boobs, but this is my show!. However, this trip to the bedroom was strictly a cash transaction. . . . How do you spell w-h-o-r-e? Yet reason prevailed—pushing a customer down the stairs would certainly bring into question her reason for being at the brothel. "Which is your room?" the man said.

One of the doors was open and she saw her luggage. "That one," she replied. Inside the room, she began peeling off her clothes.

An hour later they were back downstairs. While they were dressing he had reached over and tucked a tip into the waistband of her panties. The tip wouldn't even buy her lunch at a Sanborn's. What's worse, he had said he would recommend her to all his friends. I'll leave this episode out of my expose, she thought. Giving her no time to rest, not even time to repair her make-up, another man walked toward her with an I-want-you smile on his face. *Christ!* she thought, *How do the girls do it?* She quickly asked where she could find a bathroom and one of the girls replied, "Down the hall, next to Carmelita's room."

Ah, ha!

She found the bathroom but she walked past it to the next door. Just then a maid came out. "Is this Carmelita's room?" Lexie asked.

"Yes," the maid said. "But she's feeling poorly again. I was about to tell the last man outside she can't see anyone else tonight. I hate to do it because he's a loyal customer of hers."

I'll interview him, Lexie thought. *This is great! Tomorrow I'll slip into Carmelita's room and interview her!* "Wait!" Lexie told the maid. "I'll do Carmelita a favor. I'll take care of her customer." Once she had interviewed the man she intended to tell him she had a headache, sorry about that, and scoot him out the door.

"Oh, would you?" the maid exclaimed. "That will please Carmelita. What's your name?"

"Tell Carmelita that Lexie helped out. I'll be down in the morning to see how she's feeling."

The maid brought Carmelita's customer from the back patio into the hallway. Lexie was taken back. The man was so overly muscular that he was grotesque. He wasn't wearing a shirt for it was probably impossible to find one that fit him. His upper arms were as big around as Lexie's waist. The way the muscles in his legs quivered, even when he was standing still, his pants looked like they were filled with snakes. Every muscle in his face was developed to where his face looked like it was made from a heavy coiled rope.

"This is Alfredo," the maid said. "He's a circus strongman."

"Call me *El Gorila*," the man said.

"How about we stick with Alfredo" Lexie replied. Looking him over, she thought, *I wonder if he developed the muscles in his you-know-what as well?*

As if she had read Lexie's mind, the maid said, "Watch out, he developed the muscles in his you-know-what as well."

Alfredo said, "I get to go with this one?"

"I'm Carmelita's backup," Lexie said.

"Well what do you know?" Alfredo said, as he adjusted himself. "My lucky day."

A lesser journalist might well have tossed in the towel at this point but Lexie merely said, in that voice that inspires confidence and trust in the millions who listen to it on TV, "Let's go up to my room."

Alfredo frowned. "We aren't allowed into the main part of the house. We're considered too ugly."

"That's a house rule?" Lexie asked.

"Yes, only Carmelita entertains us ugly men."

This is getting more interesting by the minute, Lexie thought. *I'm thinking the Ortega y Gasset Prize here*! She took Alfredo by the hand. "Come on, I'm sure we can sneak upstairs without being seen."

Sure enough, they slipped into her room without being seen and Lexie closed and locked the door. She took her notebook and camera from her purse and turned to Alfredo. "Now, let me ask you a few—" But before she could finish he picked her up and tossed her onto the bed as if she weighed no more than one of the doves that his friend, the magician Senor Fantastico, pulls out of his hat. Although Alfredo's hands were as large as a bear's, his fingers were nimble and he quickly separated Lexie from her clothes. "Jesus, wait—" she started to say but by then Alfredo had his pants off and she was struck dumb by the sight of his enormous *pinga*. Recovering, she screamed, "That isn't going inside me!" and scrambled for the edge of the bed.

Alfredo pulled her back to the center of the bed then climbed between her legs. She struggled and tried to get away but he took that for playfullness. "I just want to talk," she screamed as his *pinga* forced its way into her. From then on all she could do was babble incoherently.

Alfredo was as tireless as you might expect a circus strongman to be. Hours passed—who knows how many? He didn't let up, not even pause, not even when Lexie fainted a couple of times and had to be revived with a few gentle slaps on her face. He tried everything he knew including what can only be described as "Bizarre sexual practices indigenous to circuses and carnivals." But what he liked best was simply to have her on her back with her ankles locked behind her head. This was not a position she could have achieved on her own but his strong arms bent her legs like they were cooked spaghetti. When he tired of being on top, he lifted her and placed her on top of him where she was forced to ride him like a rodeo rider on a Brahman bull. Once, when she was placed on top of him, he locked her legs behind her arms so he could spin her around. For five minutes the world was nothing but a soundless blur. It was at that time that she got the idea to do a feature on children's tops, a feature that later won her much praise.

Sometimes they stood up on the bed. Other times she was on her hands and knees (with her teeth firmly clamped on a pillow). The bed rocked back and forth so hard that it eventually broke in two and they found themselves on the floor. She closed her eyes and prayed for sleep.

When she woke the next day he was gone.

On the way to Carmelita's room she bumped into the *putanero* coming out of the kitchen. "I peeked into your room this morning," he said. "You must have had twenty men in there last night."

"It felt like it," she replied.

"Of course, I will have to deduct the repair to the bed out of your wages."

"How much will that be?" she asked.

"Who knows? It's in two pieces."

She agreed to the deduction, whatever it was.

"It seems to me a girl like you would benefit from having a strong iron brace attached to the bottom of her bed. The carpenter and I will have one installed."

"Good idea," she said.

She slipped into Carmelita's room. She introduced herself and in no time at all they were chatting like two whores who had followed Pancho Villa's army all the way from Ciudad Juarez to Mexico City and hadn't seen each other since. Lexie heard the complete story of Carmelita's life, including her account of that fateful time when one of her customers smothered to death.

"If only it had been Rudolfo with me that night," Carmelita cried. "He has two heads and one of them would have been able to breathe."

But Lexie had moved beyond that story—what's one less john in the world anyway? What if her fairy godmother had said, Lexie, I can allow you to discover one thing : A cure for aids. The formula for cold fusion. Time travel. Or the secret to breast expansion without surgery. Which one will it be? "You went from 30a to this?" Lexie said, pointing to the mounds that were Carmelita's breasts.

"Yes, but it took a few years."

Lexie reached inside her top to examine herself. She felt plumper. Was that possible? She knew deep in her heart that her imagination was probably working overtime. Still. . . . "And you could have stopped at 40d, right? I mean, if you had wanted to?" Lexie said.

Carmelita agreed that she could have.

"And you have, what? Two hundred or more customers? More than you can properly take care of?"

Carmelita agreed that that was so.

"What if some woman were to relieve you of some of your burden. Like take over fifty or sixty of your customers? Just enough of them for this woman's breasts to grow to, say, the 40d I just mentioned?"

Carmelita agreed that that would be desirable.

"I think—no, I'm definitely sure—the woman would want you to include Alfredo and any others like him."

Carmelita expressed no problem giving them up. She went on to say that the *putanero* would likely want to convert another storeroom into a second downstairs bedroom as he didn't want ugly men to be seen in the better parts of the house.

"I'm sure the woman I'm thinking about would be quite comfortable down here," Lexie said. She was thinking, *Two years at the outside*.

Carmelita smiled.

"Well, then, shall I tell the putanero that this woman is ready to take over part of your burden?"

Suddenly Carmelita was unsure. "I might miss them?" she said.

"We're only talking about 50 or 60 men."

"Still..."

"Why don't I just call the *putanero*?" She could hear pounding coming from the second floor and she assumed he was supervising the work on her bed.

"No, the more I think about it, the more I'm sure I can't give them up."

"No?"

"No."

"How about Alfredo?"

"Especially him."

"I have a confession to make," Lexie said humbly. "This won't be easy for me, but I hope that after hearing it you might reconsider? With just this one man?"

Lexie drove back to the Merida airport. Fortunately there was a late flight to Mexico City. She passed through the same villages: Buctzotz, Cansanhab, Yaxkukul. She saw Indians along the roadsides waiting for busses. This time she slowed down to avoid pelting them with stones. Alfredo fiddled with the car radio until he found a station they liked. His suitcase was within reach and he was able to find his cigarettes.

"Want me to get an iron brace for our bed?" he asked.

"Unless you like sleeping on the floor," she answered.

Lexie had decided she was going to report back that the story about Carmelita was false and that she was a girl of unremarkable size. If word got out, women would be raping ugly men in the streets. As a journalist that had some appeal, but as a competitor, in a dog-eat-dog world, why share the secret of your success?

But now wasn't the time to ponder the morality of success. Or its price, for that matter. Carmelita was successful, but her health was deteriorating. Lexie could see that the sheer weight of her breasts was preventing both her heart and lungs from functioning properly. Whores frequently die young, though, from one cause or another. Lexie knew that the real key to success, and to a long life, is to retire when you're on top—but that's easier to say than do, and she had no confidence she would fare any better at it than anyone else.

My Secret Life
Anonymous

Over two million copies sold!

Perhaps the most infamous of all underground Victorian erotica, *My Secret Life* is the sexual memoir of a well-to-do gentleman, who began at an early age to keep a diary of his erotic behavior. He continues this record for over forty years, creating in the process a unique social and psychological document. Its complete and detailed description of the hidden side of British and European life in the nineteenth century furnishes materials for the understanding of the Victorian Age that cannot be duplicated in any other source.

The Altar of Venus
Anonymous

Our author, a gentleman of wealth and privilege, is introduced to desire's delights at a tender age, and then and there commits himself to a life-long sensual expedition. As he enters manhood, he progresses from schoolgirls' charms to older women's enticements, especially those of acquaintances' mothers and wives. Later, he moves beyond common London brothels to sophisticated entertainments available only in Paris. Truly, he has become a lord among libertines.

Caning Able
Stan Kent

Caning Able is a modern-day version of the melodramatic tales of Victorian erotica. Full of dastardly villains, regimented discipline, corporal punishment and forbidden sexual liaisons, the novel features the brilliant and beautiful Jasmine, a seemingly helpless heroine who reigns triumphant despite dire peril. By mixing libidinous prose with a changing business world, *Caning Able* gives treasured plots a welcome twist: women who are definitely not the weaker sex.

The Blue Moon Erotic Reader IV

A testimonial to the publication of quality erotica, *The Blue Moon Erotic Reader IV* presents more than twenty romantic and exciting excerpts from selections spanning a variety of periods and themes. This is a historical compilation that combines generous extracts from the finest forbidden books with the most extravagant samplings that the modern erotica imagination has created. The result is a collection that is provocative, entertaining, and perhaps even enlightening. It encompasses memorable scenes of youthful initiations into the mysteries of sex, notorious confessions, and scandalous adventures of the powerful, wealthy, and notable. From the classic erotica of *Wanton Women*, and *The Intimate Memoirs of an Edwardian Dandy* to modern tales like Michael Hemmingson's *The Rooms*, good taste, passion, and an exalted desire are abound, making for a union of sex and sensibility that is available only once in a Blue Moon.

With selections by Don Winslow, Ray Gordon, M. S. Valentine, P. N. Dedeaux, Rupert Mountjoy, Eve Howard, Lisabet Sarai, Michael Hemmingson, and many others.

The Best of the Erotic Reader

"The Erotic Reader series offers an unequaled selection of the hottest scenes drawn from the finest erotic writing." — *Elle*

This historical compilation contains generous extracts from the world's finest forbidden books including excerpts from *Memories of a Young Don Juan*, *My Secret Life*, *Autobiography of a Flea*, *The Romance of Lust*, *The Three Chums*, and many others. They are gathered together here to entertain, and perhaps even enlighten. From secret texts to the scandalous adventures of famous people, from youthful initiations into the mysteries of sex to the most notorious of all confessions, *Best of the Erotic Reader* is a stirring complement to the senses. Containing the most evocative pieces covering several eras of erotic fiction, *Best of the Erotic Reader* collects the most scintillating tales from the seven volumes of *The Erotic Reader*. This comprehensive volume is sure to include delights for any taste and guaranteed to titillate, amuse, and arouse the interests of even the most veteran erotica reader.

Confessions D'Amour
Anne-Marie Villefranche

Confessions D'Amour is the culmination of Villefranche's comically indecent stories about her friends in 1920s' Paris.

Anne-Marie Villefranche invites you to enter an intoxicating world where men and women arrange their love affairs with skill and style. This is a world where illicit encounters are as smooth as a silk stocking, and where sexual secrets are kept in confidence only until a betrayal can be turned to advantage. Here we follow the adventures of Gabrielle de Michoux, the beautiful young widow who contrives to be maintained in luxury by a succession of well-to-do men, Marcel Chalon, ready for any adventure so long as he can go home to Mama afterwards, Armand Budin, who plunges into a passionate love affair with his cousin's estranged wife, Madelein Beauvais, and Yvonne Hiver who is married with two children while still embracing other, younger lovers.

"An erotic tribute to the Paris of yesteryear that will delight modern readers."—*The Observer*

A Maid For All Seasons I, II – Devlin O'Neill

Two Delighful Tales of Romance and Discipline

Lisa is used to her father's old-fashioned discipline, but is it fair that her new employer acts the same way? Mr. Swayne is very handsome, very British and very particular about his new maid's work habits. But isn't nineteen a bit old to be corrected that way? Still, it's quite a different sensation for Lisa when Mr. Swayne shows his displeasure with her behavior. But Mr. Swayne isn't the only man who likes to turn Lisa over his knee. When she goes to college she finds a new mentor, whose expectations of her are even higher than Mr. Swayne's, and who employs very old-fashioned methods to correct Lisa's bad behavior. Whether in a woodshed in Georgia, or a private club in Chicago, there is always someone there willing and eager to take Lisa in hand and show her the error of her ways.

Color of Pain, Shade of Pleasure
Edited by Cecilia Tan

In these twenty-one tales from two out-of-print classics, *Fetish Fantastic* and *S/M Futures*, some of today's most unflinching erotic fantasists turn their futuristic visions to the extreme underground, transforming the modern fetishes of S/M, bondage, and eroticized power exchange into the templates for new sexual worlds. From the near future of S/M in cyberspace, to a future police state where the real power lies in manipulating authority, these tales are from the edge of both sexual and science fiction.

The Governess
M. S. Valentine

Lovely Miss Hunnicut eagerly embarks upon a career as a governess, hoping to escape the memories of her broken engagement. Little does she know that Crawleigh Manor is far from the respectable household it appears to be. Mr. Crawleigh, in particular, devotes himself to Miss Hunnicut's thorough defiling. Soon the young governess proves herself worthy of the perverse master of the house—though there may be even more depraved powers at work in gloomy Crawleigh Manor . . .

Claire's Uptown Girls
Don Winslow

In this revised and expanded edition, Don Winslow introduces us to Claire's girls, the most exclusive and glamorous escorts in the world. Solicited by upper-class Park Avenue businessmen, Claire's girls have the style, glamour and beauty to charm any man. Graced with super-model beauty, a meticulously crafted look, and a willingness to fulfill any man's most intimate dream, these girls are sure to fulfill any man's most lavish and extravagant fantasy.

The Intimate Memoirs of an Edwardian Dandy I, II, III
Anonymous

This is the sexual coming-of-age of a young Englishman from his youthful days on the countryside to his educational days at Oxford and finally as a sexually adventurous young man in the wild streets of London. Having the free time and money that comes with a privileged upbringing, coupled with a free spirit, our hero indulges every one of his, and our, sexual fantasies. From exotic orgies with country maidens to fanciful escapades with the London elite, the young rake experiences it all. A lusty tale of sexual adventure, *The Intimate Memoirs of an Edwardian Dandy* is a celebration of free spirit and experimentation.

"A treat for the connoisseur of erotic literature."
—*The Guardian*

Jennifer and Nikki
D. M. Perkins

From Manhattan's Fifth Avenue, to the lush island of Tobago, to a mysterious ashram in upstate New York, Jennifer travels with reclusive fashion model Nikki and her seductive half-brother Alain in search of the sexual secrets held by the famous Russian mystic Pere Mitya. To achieve intimacy with this extraordinary family, and get the story she has promised to Jack August, dynamic publisher of *New Man Magazine,* Jennifer must ignore universal taboos and strip away inhibitions she never knew she had.

Confessions of a Left Bank Dominatrix
Gala Fur

Gala Fur introduces the world of French S&M with two collections of stories in one delectable volume. In *Souvenirs of a Left Bank Dominatrix*, stories address topics as varied as: how to recruit a male maidservant, how to turn your partner into a marionette, and how to use a cell phone to humiliate a submissive in a crowded train station. In *Sessions*, Gala offers more description of the life of a dominatrix, detailing the marathon of "Lesbians, bisexuals, submissivies, masochists, paying customers [and] passing playmates" that seek her out for her unique sexual services.

"An intoxicating sexual romp." —*Evergreen Review*

Don Winslow's Victorian Erotica
Don Winslow

The English manor house has long been a place apart; a place of elegant living where, in splendid isolation the gentry could freely indulge their passions for the outdoor sports of riding and hunting. Of course, there were those whose passions ran towards "indoor sports"—lascivious activities enthusiastically, if discreetly, pursued by lusty men and sensual women behind large and imposing stone walls of baronial splendor, where they were safely hidden from prying eyes. These are tales of such licentious decadence from behind the walls of those stately houses of a bygone era.

The Garden of Love
Michael Hemmingson

Three Erotic Thrillers from the Master of the Genre

In The *Comfort of Women*, the oddly passive Nicky Bayless undergoes a sexual re-education at the hands (and not only the hands) of a parade of desperate women who both lead and follow him through an underworld of erotic extremity. The narrator of *The Dress* is troubled by a simple object that may have supernatural properties. "My wife changed when she wore The Dress; she was the Ashley who came to being a few months ago. She was the wife I preferred, and I worried about that. I understood that The Dress was, indeed, an entity all its own, with its own agenda, and it was possessing my wife." In *Drama*, playwright Jonathan falls into an affair with actress Karen after the collapse of his relationship with director Kristine. But Karen's free-fall into debauchery threatens to destroy them both.

The ABZ of Pain and Pleasure
Edited by A. M. LeDeluge

A true alphabet of the unusual, *The ABZ of Pain and Pleasure* offers the reader an understanding of the language of the lash. Beginning with Aida and culminating with Zanetti, this book offers the amateur and adept a broad acquaintance with the heroes and heroines of this unique form of sexual entertainment. The Marquis de Sade is represented here, as are Jean de Berg (author of *The Image*), Pauline Réage (author of *The Story of O* and *Return to the Château*), P. N. Dedeaux (author of *The Tutor* and *The Prefect*), and twenty-two others.

"Frank" and I
Anonymous

The narrator of the story, a wealthy young man, meets a youth one day—the "Frank" of the title—and, taken by his beauty and good manners, invites him to come home with him. One can only imagine his surprise when the young man turns out to be a young woman with beguiling charms.

Hot Sheets
Ray Gordon

Running his own hotel, Mike Hunt struggles to make ends meet. In an attempt to attract more patrons, he turns Room 69 into a state-of-the-art sex chamber. Now all he has to do is wait and watch the money roll in. But nympho waitresses, a sex-crazed chef, and a bartender obsessed with adult videos don't exactly make the ideal hotel staff. And big trouble awaits Mike when his enterprise is infiltrated by an attractive undercover policewoman.

Tea and Spices
Nina Roy

Revolt is seething in the loins of the British colonial settlement of Uttar Pradesh, and in the heart of memsahib Devora Hawthorne who lusts after the dark, sultry Rohan, her husband's trusted servant. While Rohan educates Devora in the intricate social codes that govern the mean-spirited colonial community, he also introduces his eager mistress to a way of loving that exceeds the English imagination. Together, the two explore sexual territories that neither class nor color can control.

Naughty Message
Stanley Carten

Wesley Arthur is a withdrawn computer engineer who finds little excitement in his day-to-day life. That is until the day he comes home from work to discover a lascivious message on his answering machine. Aroused beyond his wildest dreams by the unmentionable acts described, Wesley becomes obsessed with tracking down the woman behind the seductive and mysterious voice. His search takes him through phone sex services, strip clubs and no-tell motels—and finally to his randy reward . . .

Order These Selected Blue Moon Titles

My Secret Life $15.95

The Altar of Venus.....................$7.95

Caning Able $7.95

The Blue Moon Erotic Reader IV $15.95

The Best of the Erotic Reader..........$15.95

Confessions D'Amour $14.95

A Maid for All Seasons I, II $15.95

Color of Pain, Shade of Pleasure........$14.95

The Governess $7.95

Claire's Uptown Girls $7.95

The Intimate Memoirs of an

Edwardian Dandy I, II, III............. $15.95

Jennifer and Nikki $7.95

Burn $7.95

Don Winslow's Victorian Erotica $14.95

The Garden of Love $14.95

The ABZ of Pain and Pleasure $7.95

"Frank" and I...........................$7.95

Hot Sheets $7.95

Tea and Spices $7.95

Naughty Message $7.95

The Sleeping Palace...................$7.95

Venus in Paris $7.95

The Lawyer $7.95

Tropic of Lust $7.95

Folies D'Amour $7.95

The Best of Ironwood $14.95

The Uninhibited $7.95

Disciplining Jane $7.95

66 Chapters About 33 Women $7.95

The Man of Her Dream $7.95

S-M: The Last Taboo..................$14.95

Cybersex $14.95

Depravicus $7.95

Sacred Exchange $14.95

The Rooms............................$7.95

The Memoirs of Josephine $7.95

The Pearl $14.95

Mistress of Instruction $7.95

Neptune and Surf $7.95

House of Dreams: Aurochs & Angels ...$7.95

Dark Star..............................$7.95

The Intimate Memoir of Dame Jenny Everleigh:

Erotic Adventures $7.95

Shadow Lane VI $7.95

Shadow Lane VII $7.95

Shadow Lane VIII $7.95

Best of Shadow Lane $14.95

The Captive I, II $14.95

The Captive III, IV, V $15.95

The Captive's Journey $7.95

Road Babe $7.95

The Story of O $7.95

The New Story of O $7.95

ORDER FORM
Attach a separate sheet for additional titles.

Title	Quantity	Price
_____	_____	_____
_____	_____	_____
_____	_____	_____
_____	_____	_____

Shipping and Handling (see charges below) _____

Sales tax (in CA and NY) _____

Total _____

Name _____

Address _____

City _____ State _____ Zip _____

Daytime telephone number _____

❏ Check   ❏ Money Order   (US dollars only. No COD orders accepted.)

Credit Card # _____ Exp. Date _____

❏ MC   ❏ VISA   ❏ AMEX

Signature _____

(if paying with a credit card you must sign this form.)

Shipping and Handling charges:*

Domestic: $4 for 1st book, $.75 each additional book. International: $5 for 1st book, $1 each additional book
*rates in effect at time of publication. Subject to Change.

Mail order to Publishers Group West, Attention: Order Dept., 1700 Fourth St., Berkeley, CA 94710, or fax to (510) 528-3444.

PLEASE ALLOW 4-6 WEEKS FOR DELIVERY. ALL ORDERS SHIP VIA 4TH CLASS MAIL.

**Look for Blue Moon Books at your favorite local bookseller
or from your favorite online bookseller.**